SUNTREE BAY

SUNTREE BAY

A Novella

AMY WORT

Print information available on the last page.

Rev. date: 09/26/2020

To order additional copies of this book, contact:
Xlibris
AU TFN: 1 800 844 927 (Toll Free inside Australia)
AU Local: 0283 108 187 (+61 2 8310 8187 from outside Australia)
www.Xlibris.com.au
Orders@Xlibris.com.au
785782

CHAPTER 1

Annabelle Delighkan sits behind the wheel of her SUV. She stares unsurely out the windscreen at an Edwardian-style house. The harsh afternoon sun makes it difficult to see the house clearly. Annabelle worryingly focuses on the house, feeling a sense of dread at the thought of entering the residence.

"Aunt Anna, what are we doing?" a young voice from behind her asks.

Annabelle snaps out of her deep daze.

"Nothing, Mitch. I'm, uh, taking you to my work now."

She starts the old Honda CR-V and allows it to drift slowly in reverse along the smooth, lengthy driveway.

The car cruises along Grand Ocean Road, which has a clear view of the vast, calm ocean. About five kilometres up the quiet road, she steers her car down into a dark underground car park. An enormous ten-storey building stands beside the car park entrance.

The dim car park is abundant with vehicles. Annabelle swings into a vacant park with the label, "Reserved for A. Delighkan." She hops out of the car, throws her butterfly handbag on her shoulder, and opens the back door. Six-year-old Mitch, wearing his green and blue uniform, sits patiently and looks at his aunty with brown innocent puppy-dog eyes as she gives him a quick smile. She unbuckles the belt and aids Mitch out of the car. Securing the vehicle, Annabelle and Mitch hold hands as they walk about ten paces to a nearby elevator. She presses the now illuminating button, and the elevator doors slide open. They board the elevator still holding hands.

The stiff air is silent. Annabelle unbuttons her handbag and pulls out a single gold key. She stares at the key, now feeling regretful she didn't enter the house.

The bulky elevator doors slide open to reveal an exquisite lobby. Annabelle and Mitch step out of their ride and onto the glossy marble floor. Straight ahead, there's a revolving door with the afternoon daylight peering in. On the left, there's an elegant curved oak staircase extending up the wall. A massive crystal chandelier with wrought-iron framing hangs as a centrepiece in the middle of the ceiling. Towards the right stands a lonely concierge desk.

Annabelle plunks her handbag on the relatively tidy desk. The hotel manager, Robert Gendrick, a fifty-year-old man wearing a smart suit and tie, approaches the desk.

"You're back so soon," Robert says in a European accent.

"Yeah, I, uh, couldn't enter the house."

"Why, couldn't you get in? Your parents did give you the key to the Delighkan House before they went on their annual holiday, seeing the family home is now rightfully yours."

"I could've easily gotten in. It's a good thing I didn't, though, because I see Pete isn't here. You know, as much as I like your son, he is slacking at his concierge training."

"Yes, well, I understand. It is rumoured to be haunted by your great-grandparents. I see why you would be a bit relucent. I just thought now would be a great time to explore the house, seeing as though the anniversary of their disappearance—as well as that of this island—is not far away."

"Shedding some light on the mystery would be grand. I promise, I'll get there."

"Very well." Robert looks down. "Nice seeing you, Mitch."

Robert walks away from the desk. Annabelle looks down at Mitch slouching against the concierge desk, which towers above him. She ruffles a pile of papers to reveal a colouring book. Then she opens a deep drawer and digs to the bottom to pull out a packet of worn-down crayons. Annabelle picks up Mitch to place him on a small clear area on the desk and hands him the book and crayons.

"Here, kid. Don't let boredom win."

Only half-enthusiastic, Mitch turns his upper body sideways so he can open the book on a flat surface. He has to flip the colouring book about four pages before he finds an uncoloured picture of a T-Rex standing beside a palm tree. The young artist begins his work.

Annabelle stands stiffly and silently, with the Delighkan House busily occupying the twenty-five-year olds mind. The sudden movement of the revolving doors blows her silky blonde hair and surprisingly clears her thoughts. A woman, close to thirty years old, with curly hair bouncing on her broad shoulders and wearing a plain white blouse and plain black pants, briskly approaches the concierge desk.

"Hello, my dear old sister. You here to pick Mitch up already? We were having so much fun," Annabelle says with a slight smile.

Wanda Remal glances at her son, who's concentrating so intently on giving the mighty looking T-Rex some colour, he doesn't even notice his mother's presence.

"Thanks for picking Mitch up from school. I just didn't know what time I was going to finish work."

"It's all right. I was out running errands anyway."

"So do you want to come around for dinner tonight? I'm making carbonara—I know you like it."

Now noticing his mother, Mitch shoves the stumpy crayons back in the packet.

"It's a date." Annabelle lifts Mitch off the desk.

"See you then. Come on, Mitch." Wanda holds out her hand for Mitch to grab.

Annabelle watches Wanda and Mitch walk towards the revolving door and eventually exit the hotel. Now, with the empty lobby before her, she finds her thoughts consumed by fear and hesitation of the Delighkan House.

Annabelle Delighkan, driving her CR-V, pulls into a flat, wide driveway. The lowset house connecting to this driveway is only half glowing, while the other half remains as a shadow outline. The rest of the houses along the quiet street appear much the same. She hops out of the car and slams the heavy door, which echoes through the soundless night. She strolls towards the almost unseen front door, only visible due to a nearby street lamp. Annabelle freely enters the Remal residence. Once inside the house, she walks into a large, dim, open room. A man, resembling a thirty-year-old version of Mitch, wears blue satin boxers and a white shirt. He sits upon the cream three-seat couch with a mobile phone in his hand. Steve Remal itches at his short facial scruff while he fidgets with his touchscreen.

"Hey, bro," Annabelle greets.

Catching his attention, Steve swivels around to see Annabelle standing just behind him. With only a quick glance, his glassy eyes make their way back to the touchscreen.

"Besides hungry, I'm pretty good."

Annabelle steps in and plops on the couch beside Steve.

"How's that ship coming along?" she asks.

Steve places his phone onto the vacant seat beside him.

"The project is coming along great. Yep, the SS *Marida* should be ready in time for the anniversary."

Wanda, wearing the same work clothes, stands on about the spot Annabelle was standing no more than a few moments ago.

"I thought I heard some commotion," Wanda says.

Steve and Annabelle swivel around to face Wanda.

"Maybe you're just hearing things," Annabelle says sarcastically.

"Dinner is ready," Wanda says, ignoring her sister's remark.

Wanda and Annabelle exit the vicinity of the lounge room. Steve follows the two sisters.

The three adults step into the neighbouring room. The dining room is bright due to the small ornamental chandelier hanging in the centre of the white ceiling. Not much occupies the partially open room, except for a plain wooden dinner table fit for six people.

Around the table sit four bowls of fettuccine carbonara. Steve, Wanda, and Annabelle are sitting in front of their plates of steamy food.

"Mitch!" Wanda yells.

Within moments, Mitch walks out from a dark hallway and sits beside his aunty. Everyone begins eating. The only sound to rattle in the ears is the forks chiming inside the half-full ceramic bowls. Annabelle looks up occasionally to see Steve and Wanda sitting opposite to her.

"So, Steve, you said the *Marida* will be ready just before the island's anniversary. Theoretically, there wouldn't be that much to do," Annabelle says.

"Well, it's a restoration project for a ship that's been out of service for twenty years, and in that time, there has been lack of maintenance."

"Hey, Wanda, aren't you writing a newspaper article about the *Marida*?" Annabelle asks as she noticeably fills with excitement.

Wanda slurps up a long bit of fettuccine.

"Yes, I am. The article is about the old ship that's been sitting in the harbour for twenty years. Also, I'm promoting the first voyage, which is the day after the anniversary."

"Hey, what jobs are you doing after the restoration?" Annabelle asks.

Steve halts on his last forkful of food.

"The upkeep on the *Marida* while she's in port. There's continuous maintenance to the ferry. Another big job is the train."

"It sounds like the two of you are busy at work these days. Whenever you need, I'm always happy to take Mitch. Gendrick is totally cool with him at the hotel."

"That's great to know because we need you to get Mitch from school tomorrow," Wanda says.

"I'm full." Mitch nudges the bowl in front of him.

"Me too, buddy. Your mum is such a good cook," Steve says.

They continue small talk for a while, letting the food settle in their stomachs.

"Do you need me to help with the dishes?" Annabelle asks.

"No, we're good. I'll walk you out now," Wanda says.

Steve stands and gathers the bowls in order to stack them. Wanda and Annabelle rise.

"I'll probably be seeing you tomorrow, Annabelle," Steve says.

"I'll see the both of you then. Goodnight."

The two women walk out of the dining room.

Wanda and Annabelle step out into the cool night air. Annabelle hops into her car and secures herself. She starts the car and winds the power window down. Wanda stands only about a foot away from the driver's door. A faint breeze cools the surrounding air.

"Thanks for taking care of Mitch," Wanda says.

"No worries, and thanks for dinner."

"No worries at all."

Annabelle begins to roll out of the driveway. The sisters exchange waves until Wanda is out of Annabelle's sight.

She drives contently along the quiet residential street. The crisp night makes the car's interior cosy. At an intersection, she pauses in her travels, hesitating whether to go left or right. She steers the car right as she makes her decision. A couple of kilometres down the road, the headlights beam against the cement driveway in the otherwise pitch-black scenery. Annabelle finds herself stationing her CR-V directly in front of the Delighkan House.

There's only absolute darkness, until she switches on the torch mode on her phone. The blinding stream of light guides her, and she pulls out the single gold key from her handbag. She chucks the bag onto the car floor and steps out of the car. She strolls up to the front door of the broken-down old house as she exhales a deep breath to brace herself. Jiggling the key in the lock, she manages to let herself in with ease.

Gently closing the door behind her, she stands in the hollow abyss. She angles her phone at eye level, revealing a slightly curved wood staircase as the centrepiece of the barely visible foyer. A little curious, Annabelle creeps towards the staircase. She grabs hold of the left-hand railing and steadily walks up, step by step.

Vivid memories of this house make her smile. Henry and Eden Delighkan were doting great-grandparents to five-year-old Annabelle, making this house a second home to the toddler. Nothing would ever slow down the one-hundred-year-old couple, who lived independently right up until the moment they disappeared. Even though they're obviously deceased, disappearing twenty years ago at the centenary age, Annabelle feels their lively presence. Warm and comforting feelings guide her slowly up the stairs. Believing in the rumour that has become the local legend, she hopes to communicate with the ghosts haunting the Delighkan House.

The empty air feels cold. Having a quick glimpse of where her delicate hand is, she notices a faint silhouette hand next to her own. Shivering with a startling fright, she shines her phone on the mysterious object. By the time white light glares off the lacquered wood, the object in focus isn't there.

A faint whisper creates an eerie sound throughout the endless silence. It would occur again about a minute later, only this time as a single distinct word.

"Henry?" a troubled feminine voice whispers.

Feeling frightful, drenched in perspiration, trembling to the knees and her heart racing, Annabelle stumbles down the stairs and towards the front door at a quick pace.

She inhales and exhales as she stands on the front porch while the bright torch is held firmly in her grip. A surprising fright continues to tremble her nerves. Still shaken, she walks on wobbly legs towards the white CR-V. Shortly after tossing her phone on the passenger seat and putting the car in drive, Annabelle disappears into the lightless night.

CHAPTER 2

It's a clear, pleasant afternoon, the sun shining warmly. A comforting breeze nudges the trees. A screechy old school bus comes to a gradual halt by the driveway to the Remal residence. Mitch steps down the steep stairs, relieved from the crowd of boisterous students, ages six through twelve. Annabelle, wearing jeans and a button top, is waiting in the driveway, leaning against the driver's door of her CR-V. Mitch runs cheerfully towards his aunty and instantly hugs her skinny waist.

"Hi, Aunt Anna." Mitch loosens his grip.

Annabelle squats down to be eye level with Mitch.

"You're going to spend the afternoon with me because your parents are working late. Any suggestions on what to do?" Annabelle asks.

Mitch tilts his head slightly to the left and scrunches up his mouth.

"Can we go on a train ride?" Mitch asks after about thirty seconds of silence.

"Okay, that would actually work because I have to go into town for something anyway."

Mitch lights up. He allows his grey oversize school bag, which hangs only from his right shoulder, to fall heavily to the concrete driveway. She picks up the school bag and tosses it on the back seat of her car. With the slam of the car door, she jolts into motion.

"Let's go," Annabelle says as she walks by and grabs his hand.

Down the concrete driveway, they begin their walking trip. Annabelle and Mitch walk along the prestige residential area, which is flowing with afternoon traffic. Reaching the borderline of the residences, they arrive at the train station. The huge open platform currently holds no more than twenty people. Annabelle stands quietly whilst still holding Mitch's hand. A cold shiver blows through her as she thinks of the Delighkan House. Mitch doesn't seem to notice Annabelle's slight shivers; he continues to stare out at the distant railway track. The train's whistle screams from afar. Annabelle snaps out of her dreadful daze as the deafening steam locomotive approaches the platform.

She watches people hop off and on the train. Mitch moves up the steep steps with Annabelle aiding him from close behind. The inside of the carriage appears much the same as the interior of a school bus—narrow aisle, two rows of seats, and large windows. Annabelle and Mitch walk along the aisle and take their seats towards the end of the carriage. The whistle sounds. Everything rattles as the locomotive is set back into motion.

The immense landscape out the window clears and soothes Annabelle's mind. The endless ocean sits calmly as the low afternoon sun glares blindingly upon the plane of water. Out the window, on the opposite side, there's a dark, dense forest. Annabelle looks back in the direction of the ocean to see Mitch squishing his face against the glass. She smiles at his happiness. The forest ends where the town begins.

Welcome to Suntree Bay. Spacious school grounds are now vacant. Up a little farther, active people of all sorts take advantage of various sporting facilities—tennis and basketball courts and a swimming pool. Circling around the keen sportspeople, the train travels the perimeter of the heart of the town.

In view, there's a whole street consisting of welcoming small businesses. The traffic along this street, both vehicles and pedestrians, seems to be at a slow pace. Travelling a little farther, there are a couple more similar-looking streets to pass by.

The train slows, and the rattling becomes less noticeable. Annabelle and Mitch continue to sit even though the train has now come to a complete halt. They watch their fellow passengers make their way out of the carriage. Annabelle stands to make their way to the exit.

Aiding Mitch down the steps, they hop onto the platform, which is identical to the one in the residential area. Grabbing Mitch's hand, they immediately walk to the edge of the platform. The vast ocean still dominates the distant landscape. The clearly visible harbour contains a large three-deck ferry and an abundance of privately moored boats. Annabelle views her silver banded watch for the time. It is a little after 4:30 p.m.

"We might as well see your mum now. She should be finishing work soon."

Wanda, wearing her black and white work gear, sits tiredly at her desk. A flat-screen computer monitor and a keyboard take up the bulk part of the desk, leaving only a quarter of the workspace for a messy pile of paperwork. She swings around effortlessly on her swivel office chair and observes the medium-size room that's full of desks set up much the same way as Wanda's desk. By now, only a couple of workers remain at these stations. Wanda swivels back around to face her blinding computer screen. Losing her thoughts, she swivels away from the screen again, this time with Annabelle and Mitch approaching. This perks her attention.

"Hello, Annabelle and my little man," Wanda greets as Mitch sinks into her arms.

"Aunt Anna took me on the train," Mitch says with a sense of excitement.

"That must have been fun." Wanda looks at her son with a smile.

"I, uh, have to talk to you about something," Annabelle says, sounding worried, "But if you're working on something, we can talk about it later."

"Now is all right. I'm nearly finished anyway."

Annabelle glances at the bright screen. Not saying a word, she wheels Wanda away from the desk. Wanda observes her sister with confusion. Annabelle bends down to face the screen. Moving the mouse, she opens the Google homepage. In the search bar, she types,

"Disappearance of Delighkans." Soon after, the computer screen displays the front page of the *Sunny Times* newspaper, dating back to the year 1993. An article is titled, "Delighkans Sea to be Missing."

"Did you go inside the Delighkan House and actually see Grandma Eden?" Wanda asks.

"No. I thought I saw a hand on the banister."

"Are you sure it wasn't your hand?"

"Unless I have two left hands, then yeah, maybe I did see Grandma Eden."

"So you're telling me that it's not just a local legend."

"I think we should go back to the Delighkan House. We can check for certain there are ghosts in that place. Also, we might be able to learn more about what happened to our great grandparents."

"What does that article say about them?" Wanda points at the screen.

Annabelle focuses on the screen as she begins to read.

"Eden and Henry Delighkan were aboard the SS *Marida* on September 3, 1993, to celebrate their eightieth wedding anniversary. They were last seen leaving the first-class dining saloon a little before 9:00 p.m." Annabelle looks up from the screen at Wanda. "That's peculiar."

"What?" Wanda looks at her sister with no interest in the matter.

"How do you go missing on a ship?"

"They must have gone overboard without anyone there to see it happen."

"I'm not convinced it's that simple. We need to dig deeper. This story has more holes than Swiss cheese."

Wanda looks at Annabelle, feeling she has the complete opposite opinion to her sister, strongly doubting the idea that there's more to this.

"I was kind of hoping the three of us could go to the Delighkan House now, if it's not a burden," Annabelle says.

Wanda knows how close Annabelle was to her great-grandparents as a kid, even though she didn't have the same connection. Noticing how shaken up Annabelle is about the scenario, Wanda agrees to go. She shuts down her computer, stands, and throws her oversize handbag onto her shoulder. Annabelle grabs Mitch's hand.

"You know, you can keep him if you want."

Annabelle raises her eyebrow as she accepts the statement as a joke. The sisters and Mitch walk away from the desk. Wanda is now the last worker to leave.

"You must be putting in some overtime," Annabelle says.

They approach the elevator, and Wanda presses the button.

"Well, I am covering the front-page story. Besides, lack of resources is holding me back a bit."

"Who knows, you might learn a thing or two about the *Marida* while we're at the house."

Everyone steps into the vacant elevator. With only a quick drop in altitude the elevator doors slide open to reveal a pretty ordinary office building lobby. They step out of the elevator and walk past a fern and a two-seat sofa. Wanda's stilettos tapping on the glossy vinyl floor echo through the hall. A near-empty water cooler stands against a nearby wall. The huge reception desk sits to the side with a clear view of the building's entrance. The receptionist, a young man in a suit, is the only other person in the area.

"See you tomorrow, Wanda," the receptionist says.

"See you then. Have a good night."

Annabelle pushes the heavy glass door and holds it open for Wanda and Mitch. The large, next-to-empty car park is directly outside the lobby. Wanda, Annabelle, and Mitch walk about halfway up the bare tar until they reach a Toyota Corolla sedan. With the click of a button, the car unlocks, and Annabelle hops into the passenger seat. Wanda helps Mitch into his booster seat, throws her bag beside him, and hops in the driver's seat. The car's interior is still warm from being under the sun all day. She starts the quiet engine and glides the car to the car park's exit.

Wanda keeps her attention forward as she drives through the town. Traffic flow is low now due to the local businesses reaching the end of the day. The low-hanging sun makes direct eye contact with Wanda, forcing her to pull down the visor.

"Are you sure it's all right coming into the Delighkan House with me?" Annabelle asks.

"Yes, its fine, Annabelle," Wanda says, sounding irritated after being asked for the umpteenth time.

"That's good because I'm still not sure what I actually saw last night."

Wanda quickly glimpses over at her sister, who's now looking out the window. She turns her attention back to the road, hoping that Annabelle did encounter the alleged ghost and is not crazy. The Corolla travels along the long, smooth driveway and arrives in front of the Delighkan House. Wanda hops out of the car and then aids Mitch. By the time Wanda and Mitch arrive at the doorstep, Annabelle is already there. The feeling of uncertainty suddenly washes over Wanda as she watches Annabelle turn the single gold key in the stiff lock. The door creaks open. The sisters and Mitch step into the foyer.

The dimming sun beams faintly through the huge, dusty window and into the hollow area. The curved wooden staircase is the centrepiece. The archway on the left leads to an increasingly darkening room. Wanda approaches the staircase and walks up a couple of creaky steps. She rests her left hand on the banister. Seeing no ghost revealing itself, Wanda remains sceptical about the concept.

"So this is where you thought you saw Grandma Eden?" Wanda says.

"Well, a few more steps up, but, yeah, generally."

"There's definitely nothing here, proving that the idea of this house being haunted is fiction, not fact."

"Don't be so closed-minded. I know she's here."

Wanda shakes her head, disagreeing with Annabelle's opinion.

"I know where she might be."

Annabelle races up the stairs. Wanda looks down at Mitch at the base of the staircase. She steps down, grabs his hand, and walks up the stairs with him. Annabelle is standing at the top of the staircase.

"It sounded like this was the spot Grandma Eden called out to Grandpa Henry," Annabelle says.

"Oh, so you're hearing voices now," Wanda says with a smirk.

Annabelle turns to the right and slowly disappears down the hall. Wanda and Mitch follow her. Annabelle turns to the left with Wanda and Mitch closely behind. Henry and Eden's bedroom is of moderate size, with their double-size ensemble bed being the central feature. Wanda remains in the doorway as Mitch brushes past her.

"Well, there seems to be no ghosts in this place, so are we right to go now?" Wanda asks.

Annabelle approaches one of the pine bedside tables. There's a large lamp and a small hardcover book with a thick coat of dust on the table. Mitch stands beside Annabelle as she delicately picks up the small hardcover book and plonks herself on the edge of the bed. Wanda decides to step into the room and sits beside her. Opening the hardcover, Annabelle reads aloud the three lines of tiny fancy handwriting:

Journal of
Eden Ainsley-Delighkan
I write this journal to capture the moments
I travel and explore this vast world.

"Are you going to read us a story, Aunt Anna?" Mitch asks.

"With the centenary anniversary of Suntree Bay less than a month away, it'll be a great time to learn some insight into the beginning of the island. Also, I guarantee this journal will mention the *Marida*," Annabelle says.

"It could even mention something to do with Grandpa Henry and Grandma Eden disappearing twenty years ago."

"I don't think it's going to give away all its secrets, but one can only hope we will discover clues that might lead to the truth about their disappearance."

"Well, let's get on with it then."

"It's good to see you're finally intrigued."

"Hey, they were my great-grandparents too; I'm just not buying into the whole ghost part of it."

Wanda gestures to Mitch with open arms. The young boy sits on his mother's lap. Annabelle flips the page and begins reading the handwritten passage aloud.

May 2, 1911, 08.00

Today I am an adventurous girl beginning my journey sailing upon the horizon and arriving on the shores of the new world. Even though this is my first time leaving Queenstown, Ireland, New York City is easily set in my sight.

Eden Ainsley sits stiffly on the wooden deck chair. The faint early morning sun glares down and creates a thermal through her long-hanging long-sleeved dress. She squints while writing in her small hardcover journal, which is tightly in her grip on her dainty lap.

"Hello there, ma'am," an Irish man says.

Eden looks up to find a young man wearing a grey suit, complete with a tie and a vest hidden behind a button coat. She closes her journal while maintaining eye contact with the strikingly handsome man.

"You must be enthused to arrive in New York, seeing that you're on the boat deck of the SS *Marida* four hours before departure."

"I love ships, which I owe to the gratitude of seeing my father sailing off ever since I can remember," Eden says.

"Allow me to introduce myself. I'm Henry Delighkan, one of the architects of this very fine ship."

"I love your work. This ship looks magnificent."

"Thank you. I owe the dedication to the hard workers in Belfast, for the designing and building of the *Marida* and a soon-to-come sister ship. So is Captain Martin Ainsley your father?"

"He sure is. Pardon me for saying, but you seem quite young to be designing ships."

Henry sits on the neighbouring deck chair. Eden subtly stares at Henry, curious to learn more about the man with the association to the shipping industry.

"I'm flattered. I just turned eighteen only last month. I'm an apprentice at the moment, so, basically, I'm a designer in the making. My friend Thomas has mentored my growing passion for architecture. One of his ships is actually being launched in about three weeks," Henry says.

"That's lovely. Would you believe I turned eighteen last month also?"

"I would believe that to be a coincidence."

Eden smiles while she unnoticeably begins to blush. She feels easy and comfortable in the presence of Henry. He pulls out his gold fob watch from his jacket pocket, which has a chain attaching the watch to his clothing. He notices the time and quickly places the watch back in the pocket.

"I'm sorry, but I need to excuse myself. I was on my way to talk to Captain Ainsley, but I'm glad I talked to you first, Miss Ainsley." Henry rises to his feet. "I hope to see you again soon."

"That would be lovely."

"Good day to you."

Henry walks off. Eden watches Henry walk along the wooden deck with a warm, fuzzy feeling growing inside her. With a glowing smile, she drops her attention back down into her journal.

May 2, 1911, 08:15

I feel somewhat honoured to meet one of the gentlemen responsible for the ship I shall sail upon. I am grateful to have met such an upstanding man. Today, a new chapter is opening up in my life, and I feel a sense of change beyond the upcoming horizon.

The spacious bridge of the SS *Marida* is bright as the midday sun beams through the large forward-facing glass window. Captain Ainsley stands close to this window as he observes his fellow crew. The young sailor in his navy blue uniform and white hat, looking a bit like Popeye the Sailor Man, firmly grips the wooden helm, which stands only about a foot shorter than the lean man. Chief Officer Berg, wearing a black suit and tie with gold bands around the wrists of the jacket and a hat resembling a captain's hat, makes direct eye contact with Captain Ainsley as he stands on the far end of the bridge's window. First Officer Townsen, dressed identically to Chief Officer Berg, approaches the telegraph, a golden cylindrical item with a lever on the top.

"Get ready to communicate with the engine room, Townsen," Captain Ainsley says.

"Yes, sir," Townsen says, standing stiffly.

Captain Ainsley's attention drifts out to the water beyond the lengthy bow. He watches on as two tiny tugboats serve their purpose, slowly tugging the SS *Marida* by separate thick, durable ropes.

A middle-aged man stands on the dock only a couple of feet away from the ship. He stares silently in awe as the ship, as tall as an eight-storey building, begins to float away from the cheery crowded dock. The SS *Marida* appears much like a miniature version of the RMS *Titanic*, with rows of portholes running along the over-five-hundred-foot-long hull, white railings wrapping around and the mast, standing tall about a couple of metres away from the lonely smokestack. Black smoke blows out from the smokestack as the ship's whistle blows. By now, the *Marida* is about ten feet away from the man. With the help of the two tugboats and the waking of the *Marida*'s inner power, the magnificent ship glides towards the open sea.

CHAPTER 3

The room is exquisite. White light beams through the crystal dome light shade, making the smooth oak walls gloss. The warmth from the wooden mantelpiece, with a wavy golden border and containing an electric heater, delivers a cosy feel to the square room. The wooden box clock with its Roman numeral face behind glass, sits in the middle of the mantelpiece. Its delicate hands reveal that it is nearly six o'clock.

In the centre of the comfortably fit room, there's a small circular table. Four softly padded chairs surround the table. Only one of these chairs is resting a bottom, as Eden sits upright, facing forward. Looking impressively well, she's wearing an emerald dress that drapes down to the floor. Her tight corset is hidden underneath, pushing her petite breasts upward. Eden's thick blonde hair is arranged neatly in a loose bun.

A young lady, just a little older than Eden, enters the quiet sitting room. She wears a plain navy blue dress that just about covers her entire body, the front part protected by a white lace apron. Her freckled face gleams under the dazzling light as she approaches Eden. Eden looks up at the maid with gladness.

"I saw this in your jewellery box and thought it would look nice." The maid reveals a gold chain necklace with a ruby stone pendant.

"Thanks, Molly. It's a great choice."

Molly drifts behind Eden and slips the thin golden chain around her bare neck. The ruby stone is now the centrepiece of Eden's half-naked chest. She bends forward and pulls the neighbouring chair away from the table. Molly moves back in front of Eden and hesitantly sits down.

"Sit with me, at least until my father arrives," Eden says.

"Are you excited for New York City?"

"Very much so. A new journey in a new country. I am looking forward to it."

A gentle three-tap knock at the nearby door barely stirs Eden. Molly's immediate reaction is to spring off her comfy seat, approach the door, and open it to reveal the visitor. It's Captain Ainsley, dressed formally, as always, in his black captain's uniform. He stands stiff, with his hard maintain in shape hat snug underneath his left arm.

"Good evening, Captain Ainsley," Molly greets as she moves to the side of the doorway.

"Good evening, Molly." Accepting the welcoming gesture, Martin enters the stateroom. Molly softly closes the door behind Martin. He makes himself comfortable by gracefully sitting upon the chair Molly once sat on.

"I'll leave you two alone, then."

Molly exits the room. Martin views his daughter with a smile as she expresses contentment and excitement.

"What is it, Father?"

"I'm just glad that you're happy. Being eighteen years old and travelling to a foreign country, and with half your family back home. It's a new outlook."

"I know, Father. I also know that the world is bigger than Queenstown, and I'm keen to explore it."

"Perfect attitude." Martin rises to his feet and holds out his hand towards Eden. "Shall we go to dinner?"

Eden swiftly stands up and takes her father's hand. They exit the stateroom together. The narrow corridor is bright due to the tiny brass and crystal light fixtures running along both walls. The carpet runner cushions every step. An elderly man wearing a tuxedo walks by and quickly greets the Ainsleys.

It's only a short walk down the corridor until Martin and Eden reach the large B-deck staircase. The polished oak walls beam under the bright artificial light coming from the massive crystal chandelier. The huge curved oak staircase sits slightly to the right, which meets with an overhanging balcony. In the centre of the wall, on Eden's left, there's a Roman numeral grandfather clock encased in the wall with pendulums gently swaying. Continuing on, Martin and Eden walk under a wide white glossy archway.

They enter the room with intertwined arms. The dining saloon is an elegant room to dine and mingle. Thin and white decadent columns about ten feet apart connect the barely visible carpeted floor to the finely detailed carved pattern ceiling. Twenty-five dining tables are evenly placed among the spacious area. The middle tables can seat about ten people, while the smaller tables around the outskirts of the room seat about four. Every table, however, is set with a white lace tablecloth, which droops about halfway down the tables' pine legs. Glossy crockery at each individual placing has freshly polished cutlery by its side. First-class men and women, dressed in their best formal attire, flood around the tables. Soft band music soothes the air. The small chandeliers brighten the scenery.

The captain escorts his daughter to a middle table, where two gentlemen are already in their seats.

"It's nice to see you again, Henry," Eden says.

"Yes, it's nice seeing you again too," Henry says.

"I see you're already acquainted with my daughter," Martin says.

Eden looks at the other gentleman. He's about midforties, his black hair shiny, with a few odd grey hairs visible. His neatly bushy moustache on his pale upper lip makes him appear that slightly older than he is.

"I believe I haven't had the pleasure. I'm Louis Fisher, the chairman of Blue Ocean Line."

"Oh yes, the shipping company that owns the SS *Marida*," Eden says.

Martin pulls out a chair for Eden to rest her dainty bottom. He pulls out the neighbouring chair to rest upon.

"My daughter, Eden, is quite interested in ships."

"Growing up in Belfast, my father was the owner of a shipyard. I've always been interested in ships as well," Henry says.

"Your father is a great man, and he speaks highly of you. Ever since 1895, I've never regretted the decision of choosing Delighkan Shipyard to build Blue Ocean Line ships," Louis says.

"I'm flattered to hear that," Henry says.

Eden looks at Henry with a subtle smile. Henry appears to have his attention on something beyond the table before him. His gaze drifts as Eden sees an elderly couple approach Captain Ainsley from behind. Eden looks at the couple in awe while they hold hands as the gentleman helps his wife into the seat beside the captain.

"That's true love," Henry says.

Eden swings her attention back to Henry. She feels warm on the inside after observing the elderly couple and hearing Henry's remark. A plump man with a receding hairline approaches Louis Fisher from behind and sits in the vacant chair beside him.

"Hey, Fisher, I haven't seen you for a while," the man says.

"It must be a small world to bump into you on a ship in the Atlantic, Timothy," Louis says.

"Yes, and on a tiny ship."

"Don't speak ill of my associate's ship." Louis points at Henry with his thumb. "He's on his way to proving to be a fine architect," Louis says.

"You must work for Delighkan Shipyard. I'm not speaking ill. I find this ship to be quite luxurious," Timothy says.

"Yes, I'm Henry, Edward Delighkan's son." Henry stretches his arm in front of Louis to shake hands with Timothy. "Louis is exaggerating. I'm only an apprentice in a team with at least eight other men, so only a small portion of my creativity went into the SS *Marida*. My three brother's work went into this vessel more so than mine. They're all shipbuilders for my father's company."

"Positivity is what pushes us forward. Positive talk from Louis is part the reason I now own an oil company."

Eden can tell the praise about Henry is overwhelming him, as he begins to faintly blush. Six waiters wearing white suits place meals in front of the chatty occupants of the table. Eden whispers a thank-you as a waiter places a meal in front of her. The scrumptious red meat fillet and roast vegetables let out wisps of steam. Eden doesn't immediately begin to eat; she continues listening to the conversation without saying a word.

"So, Louis, how is your family?" Timothy asks.

"They're going well at home in Queenstown. The eldest child started university earlier this year," Louis says.

The chattering lowers as everyone begins to eat. Eden every so often looks up from her food and observes her fellow diners. Timothy gulps down his mouthful of food.

"So you're a promising architect with a hopeful career. Why are you leaving Ireland, Henry?" Timothy asks.

"I'm not gone for long. I just thought it would be an educational experience to explore a steam liner in service; also, it's an opportunity to explore the world beyond Belfast."

A brief moment passes without any talking. The chattering from the other tables fills the room's atmosphere.

"Captain Ainsley, how's the family?" Timothy asks.

"My wife is a little under the weather getting over the flu, with one daughter there helping her out. Eden seems content while aboard this vessel. I believe she's travelling for similar reasons as Henry," Captain Ainsley says.

Eden smiles as the men at the table give her quick glances.

"Well, then, I suppose I better return to the bridge." Captain Ainsley stands. "Would you like me to escort you back to your cabin, Eden?"

"I can accompany Eden, if she's fine with that," Henry says.

"That's very kind of you," Eden says.

"Very well. Good evening, gents—and Eden." Captain Ainsley leaves. Timothy stands.

"It must be cigar and brandy time."

"I agree," Louis says, standing as well. "You're welcome to join us, Henry."

"I think I might retire for the evening after accompanying Eden."

Louis and Timothy say goodnight and leave. Eden turns her head to the left to see that the elderly couple are the only other people at the table. They keep their chattering amongst themselves. Waiters begin clearing the table.

"Would you care for some dessert?" Henry asks.

"That sounds lovely, thank you."

"Excuse me, sir." Henry catches the attention of a middle-aged waiter as he leans across the table for a plate.

"Yes, sir," the waiter says.

"May I burden you for two slices of cake?"

"Certainly, sir."

The waiter walks away. Eden glances at Henry from across the table. She gleams with appreciation at the kindness put forward by the young gentleman.

"So I suppose you are only vacationing in New York. I'm only asking because your mother and sister remain in Ireland," Henry says.

The same middle-aged waiter returns and places two slices of sponge cake with a generous swirl of whipped cream on the side in front of Henry and Eden. They both say thank you as the waiter smiles and walks away.

"My father and I are only in New York for about a month. Then, my father is commanding the RMS *Mystic* from New York to Liverpool. I guess that's when I'll return home."

"I've heard of the *Mystic*. I saw it advertised three years ago, just before its maiden voyage. I recall it being owned by Gemsant, a Canadian company."

"Are you remaining in New York once the ship is docked?" Eden asks.

"I'm actually heading to Canada and staying there for about two weeks before shipping back to Ireland. After admiring pictures of the Canadian wilderness, my father thought it would be in my favour to vacation there once my observation with the *Marida* was done with."

"That sounds fun."

Henry and Eden pick up shiny cake forks and begin eating their sweet treat. They quietly savour their bites. Eden looks up from her food. She looks at Henry with a sense of trust and feels as though she can comfortably confide her whole world to him. Henry looks back at her with a smile. She shoves a forkful of cake in her mouth, smearing some of the whipped cream just above her lip.

"You are not like any other lady I've met," Henry says with a soft chuckle.

Eden doesn't react at all to the cool cream against her skin. Henry picks up a large cloth napkin and wipes her upper lip. Eden begins to feel the warmth of her blush in a moment that seems to last an eternity. Henry places the napkin neatly on the table. He scrapes up the last little piece of sponge cake with his fork. Eden is at least two bites behind.

"Am I keeping you from your personal matter?" Eden asks.

"Not at all. I was only going to retire to my room and read."

Eden takes her last bite and swallows the contents.

"The idea of getting lost in someone's fictional world and connecting with characters—I find it quite an enjoyable way to spend my free time."

"I quite enjoy the concept myself," Eden says.

Henry pulls out his fob watch and glimpses at it.

"Shall we?"

Eden stands. Henry stands and walks around the table. He holds out his bent arm, ready to escort Eden.

"Lead the way, miss."

They begin moving towards the arch exit. The dining saloon is still lively thanks to the cheery chattering folk remaining at the tables.

Henry and Eden make their way past the B-deck staircase and continue a short distance up the corridor. Eden stops at her door.

"This is me."

"Would you believe I'm in the very last room along this same corridor?" Henry says.

"I believe fate would have it."

"Now that you know where to find me. Don't hesitate if you need anything."

"Thank you and goodnight." Eden opens the door and steps inside.
"Goodnight, ma'am." Henry leaves.

The comforting sense that Henry is only a short distance away brings a smile to Eden's face as she closes the door.

May 5, 1911, 16:15

The SS Marida and I are no longer maidens in terms of sailing upon the open ocean. The past four days travelling on the calm blue have been quite relaxing—no hiccups, to say the least.

Eden sits in a comfy half-dome chair, with a huge window beside her, the light glaring through. Her only company is her hardcover journal, which she holds tightly in her grip as she busily writes on a clean empty page. In terms of decor, this reading and writing room mirrors Eden's stateroom, except that it is larger. A few other young ladies in the room act similar to Eden, sitting quietly with only a book as their company.

She ceases writing and slowly moves around to glance out the window closest to her. Within seconds, she repositions her body upright in the chair and continues to write.

The haunting clouds that are looming dangerously close worry me a little. Henry Delighkan, the gentleman that he is, has ensured me there is no need to worry.

Eden springs to her feet. With her journal in her hands, she approaches the window. She presses against the cold, hard glass and stares out to the horizon. Thick navy blue clouds bury the sun and dominate much of the grey sky. The surface of the endless ocean gradually begins to form small, peaky waves. Threatening weather looms. She gives the outside landscape one last look before walking towards the archway exit. Eden steps up the C-deck staircase. Completing her ascent, she pops out from behind the staircase on B-deck. She calmly continues down the corridor until she reaches the end. Eden taps on the door a few times. The door opens to reveal Henry.

"Hello, Miss Ainsley. Anything the matter?"

"The upcoming weather is worrying me a little."

Just looking at Henry makes Eden's negative thoughts and feelings disappear.

"Would you like to go out on deck with me?" Henry asks.

"Yes, I would love to."

Henry steps out of his room and closes the door. They walk down the corridor. In the B-deck stairwell, they continue up the stairs and onto A-deck, exiting through a wood-framed glass door. As she steps out onto the wide-open deck, the threatening weather stretches across the horizon straight ahead.

"It does look just that wee bit of a worry, but I can assure you that your father is a great captain. Should something hit, he'll do his very best to keep everyone onboard safe," Henry says.

"Storms fascinate me, but they concern me."

They gaze out at the ominous sky as the clouds get heavier.

The bridge of the SS *Marida* is a quiet place. A young sailor firmly holds the helm. Captain Ainsley stands beside the sailor. Both men look out through the large window beyond the bow and at the open sea. Dark, monstrous clouds, appearing even darker than, before gradually drawing closer. Chief Officer Berg approaches the captain.

"Sir, these clouds are getting closer. What shall we do?" Chief Officer Berg asks.

"Decrease speed to around ten knots and telegram any nearby ships about the approaching storm. It appears this storm is heading in a northerly direction, so I reckon we should travel farther south. By doing so, we should only be grazed by the weather."

"Yes, sir," Chief Officer Berg replies, and he leaves to carry out his duties.

Martin turns his attention back to the dangerous-looking horizon, confident he has taken the right course of action.

In the dining saloon, Captain Ainsley, Louis, Henry, and Eden are sitting around the huge central table. Waiters come around to remove their empty plates. Henry stands and walks around to Eden to take her hand as he helps her to her feet.

"Mr. Delighkan, thank you for treating my daughter well. It's nice to see she has company," Captain Ainsley says happily.

"It's my pleasure, Captain."

"Good night, Father." Eden gives her father a peck on the cheek.

Henry and Eden, with arms entwined, depart from the table. Captain Ainsley and Louis Fisher remain across from each other at the empty table.

"Well, then, excuse me. I had better return to the bridge."

"How is the weather situation, Captain?"

"I can ensure you there's nothing to worry, just act like the passenger that you are and have confidence in me and my crew. Goodnight, Mr. Fisher."

Henry escorts Eden out of the dining saloon through the archway. They walk up the stairs to A-deck and towards the wooden frame glass door. The wide open deck is quiet and cool. The night sky blankets like a dark abyss. The SS *Marida* beams brightly as she gracefully steams ahead on the placid sea. Eden focuses her attention immediately on the pitch-black landscape that stretches before her.

"May I ask why you desire to come out on deck?" Henry asks.

Eden maintains her deep eye contact with the dark scenery. She feels the spirit of the storm as she observes it intently.

"I feel the weather."

Henry loosens his grip and breaks the stance with her. She snaps out of her trance at the weather and faces him. Henry slowly bends in and indulges in a sweet kiss. Eden closes her eyes as the passion empties her mind, allowing her to savour the seemingly endless moment. A violent roar of thunder vibrates the ship down to its keel. They tear away from their kiss.

A blinding strike of lightning meets the horizon, turning night into day. Like an earthquake shaking a building, mighty waves throw the powerless ship up and down with tremendous force. The beautiful terror of the storm reclaims Eden's attention as she hears the deafening thunder. *Bang!* A second strike of lightning meets the horizon, this time briefly revealing the shape of a large object in the far distance. The fresh smell of rain lingers through the air only seconds before heavy droplets begin to pelt down on the deck. As the thunder, lightning, waves, and rain continue their symphony, Henry grabs Eden's hand and leads her to enter back through the door. Eden once again snaps out of the hypnotic state caused by the storm. They grip onto the bottom end of the nearby oak banister.

"Thank you. I'm sorry I got a little carried away," Eden says.

"It's OK. We're safe now."

Lights in the stairwell dim and flicker. Besides the young couple, there's no one in this area. Eden tightly hugs the banister as she feels the floor underneath turning to an upward angle. Weighty rain droplets make cracking sounds as they smack against the wood-framed glass door. The floor levels off, and it is now safe to stand on. Eden lets go of the banister. Suddenly, a shockwave passes through the *Marida* as it crashes into something. This knocks Eden off her feet. She lies flat on her back on the cold, hard floor.

"Are you all right?" Henry lets go of the banister. A sudden vibration startles Eden.

Annabelle throws Eden's journal on a nearby pillow, stands up, and pulls her vibrating phone out of her jeans pocket. She adjusts her eyes to the small glaring screen. The rest of the room is dully lit; the sun is gone, and only the last fragment of daylight remains.

"Hello," she answers her phone.

Wanda and Mitch listen curiously. Annabelle's clear voice amplifies throughout the house.

"Sorry, we uh, are still at Wanda's office. She really gets into her work, but sometimes, she does need help from her sister." She pauses. "Yeah, Mitch is here. Don't worry. They both should be home soon. Bye." Annabelle hangs up the phone. She shoots a confused look towards Wanda as if to say, "Why is your husband ringing me to find you?"

"My phone is sitting in the car," Wanda says.

"I suppose it's time to head off. My eyes are starting to feel the strain from reading in this dim light."

Wanda rises stiffly to her feet.

"Come on, Mitch, it's time to go home," Wanda says as she watches her son slide off the side of the bed.

Wanda, Annabelle, and Mitch leave the increasingly darkening room.

CHAPTER 4

Annabelle stands by her kitchen sink, staring at the darkness that lurks outside the window. She dunks her red hands in the soapy water and reaches for the plug. Swishing the water to eliminate the excess soap suds, she accidently splashes some dishwater on the floor. Sighing, she shakes her wet hands, lights up the laundry next to the kitchen, and opens a narrow cupboard. Reaching past a bulky old lantern hanging on a hook, she grabs the mop from its bucket and wipes the water off the floor.

Annabelle leans the mop against a nearby wall, then sits at the diminutive round kitchen table. Glancing down at her mobile phone, she decides to pick it up and place a call. She allows the phone to ring out until a famine voice states, "Not here to pick up the phone." A beep follows.

"Hi, Mum. Hope you and Dad are enjoying your holiday. Talk to you soon. Bye." She hangs up the phone.

She stands up and grabs the mop to place it back in the cupboard. Bumping the lantern with the handle end of the mop and brings her attention to the metallic object. Thinking of the lovely journal tale from the past makes Annabelle completely forget about the present haunting, and seeing the lantern makes her wanting to read more. She grabs the lantern off the hook and switches off the light on her way out of the laundry. Annabelle bends to retrieve a packet of matches from the bottom drawer in the kitchen. She leaves the kitchen and heads for the door, turning lights off on the way.

Annabelle then exits her little unit. She walks down about three cement stairs and towards her CR-V under a tin carport, directly in front of her dark unit. Abundant light protrudes from the other four units in the complex. The only light to aid Annabelle at the car is one street light standing about ten feet away. The odd car zooms by, shining its headlights like a spotlight gleaming on a stage. Annabelle fiddles in the semi-darkness as she fishes her keys out of her bag and hops in the car. She places the lantern on the passenger seat. The hard slam of the car door echoes throughout the carport, followed by the car's ignition. Annabelle rolls the car down the short yet steep driveway. With a bit of a turn, the humming SUV is in pursuit of her travels along the spot-lit street.

Passing only a few houses, she reaches a four-way intersection and turns right. The vacant train station with a lonely light beaming on the platform sits on the left, a fair distance from the road. A new car with eye-torturing LED headlights drives past, making Annabelle squint. She passes several more houses and straight through an intersection. Another car slowly drives by, this time with dull headlights.

Now on the fringe of the neighbourhood, Annabelle inches up the smooth, lengthy driveway. Her headlights shine against the Delighkan House as she switches the car off, leaving her in quiet darkness. Stepping out of the car with her handbag on her shoulder and the lantern in her hand, she briefly looks up to admire the clear starry sky. The crescent moon provides just enough light to approach the front door. Pulling out the key and unlocking it, Annabelle welcomes herself into the eerie house. She pulls out the matches from her handbag and then dumps the bag by the front door as though she lives here. She lights the lantern, and the dim glow illuminates a nearby archway. Annabelle slowly steps forward into what seems like a black hole.

As she walks through the lounge room, it becomes clear that the household hasn't seen any occupants for quite some time. A three-seater couch ending with chunky arm rests makes you wonder what its fabric used to look like, not only because of the thick coating of grey dust but also because of the complex formations of cobwebs. The barely noticeable couch faces the old television set, which takes up the entire surface space of a small TV unit. The room seems so spacious, being that this area is taken by just one more piece of furniture—a wooden bookcase with glass doors. As far as Annabelle can see, it's filled with ceramic ornaments, but the glare from the lantern makes it hard to see anything in detail. Observing that everything in this lounge room seems to date back to the 1990s, Annabelle steps back out to the foyer.

Coming out from the lounge room, Annabelle turns to her left. She ventures beyond the dominating staircase and finds an archway on her right. She continues on into the abyss. Shining her fiery lantern into this room, she finds books lining three of the walls and a dusty chalkboard standing in the corner. The object that really grabs her attention is a massive desk, about five feet across, and the central area of the room. She makes herself comfortable at the pine desk by sitting upon a high-back swivel chair. She places her glowing lantern on the corner of the desk.

Annabelle's curiosity is aroused by the messy array of papers, which almost appear like a tablecloth covering the surface of the desk. She's particularly curious about a twenty-page booklet which has a two-line cover page that reads, "Charley Star" with "Written by Eden Delighkan" directly underneath. As she is about to pick up the booklet, a gargling cough shrieks from outside the office. Annabelle snatches the lantern and rushes out of the room. In the foyer, she takes a deep breath to calm her nerves. There's no one and nothing seemingly present. Annabelle stands in the middle of the foyer, curious about the sound. A cold chill causes her to shiver. It feels as though a draft is coming from the direction of the staircase. She walks towards the base of the staircase and ventures up, grabbing the railing.

After a bit of a curvy walk upward, she finds herself entering the first room she comes across, which is Henry and Eden's bedroom. Eden's journal lying open on the bed immediately comes to Annabelle's attention. She picks up the journal.

"This is the reason why I came here. I know just the place to continue my reading."

With the open journal in her hand, Annabelle exits the bedroom and walks back down the stairs. Walking along, she enters the office and makes herself comfortable at the desk.

May 6, 1911, 07:30

*Though I am not familiar with the Transatlantic Lane,
it seems my father has driven the Marida farther south
than he was supposed to. The tropical beauty that I admire
is a new world to me. Coming from Queenstown, I am not
used to this warmer climate.*

The young sky welcomes a fine day; the vast sea lies calm, and the radiant sun shines just above the horizon. Chattering crowds gather on the bow and boat deck on the lifeless *Marida*. Captain Ainsley, Berg, Louis, and Henry stand just outside the bridge. Eden stands only a couple of steps away.

"Berg, tell the wireless operators to message any nearby ships for assistance," Captain Ainsley orders.

"Yes, sir," Berg says, walking away.

"Even though it would be bad publicity, being the maiden voyage and all, my best guess is the *Marida* needs to be towed back to Belfast," Louis says.

"Certainly, and I think this is a good learning experience for Henry."

"Yes, we can lower you down in a lifeboat, and you can inspect the damage to the bow."

"OK." Henry pushes through the crowd as he walks towards the nearby wooden lifeboat.

"Eden should go down also," Captain Ainsley says.

Eden's ears perk up at the mention of her name. She follows the three men to the lifeboats, which are in rows along the boat deck. Two young sailors, about Henry's age, approach the davits, a small crane on either side of the boat. They begin pulling at thick ropes which weave through the davit and attach to the ends of the lifeboat. With hoist on the ropes, the davits swing the lifeboat over the side of the *Marida*. Henry hops in and assists Eden in coming aboard. The sailors lower the lifeboat. After descending for about five minutes, the lifeboat touches the sandy ground. Henry hops out of the boat and then helps Eden out. Rough ocean swells swish about halfway up the lifeboat. The salty sea breeze blows through. Henry immediately walks along the *Marida* until he reaches the very tip of the bow. Eden wanders in the same direction as Henry. A boulder about the size of a tugboat presses against a buckle in a section of the bow. Eden looks at the bow for a short moment before her attention drifts towards the land.

Towering trees grow in endless abundance. The neighbouring beach, with its golden gleaming sand, carries on from the vegetation in a virtually straight line, like a barrier. The early morning sun beams upon the island, highlighting the beautiful landscape.

"When we felt that crash last night, it was this boulder that prevented us from going any further," Henry says.

Eden looks briefly at Henry, then turns her attention back to the tropical paradise before her. Henry turns around to view the scene.

"The only thing I find more beautiful than this scenery is you, Eden."

They look at each other. The remark gives Eden butterflies in her stomach.

"Are you ready to come back aboard, Mr. Delighkan?"

They look up to find Louis peering over the bow railing.

"Yes, sir. We will make our way back on the boat."

The whipping wind grows more forceful while the choppy ocean becomes angry. Eden reaches the bow of the lifeboat before Henry. As she stands beside the boat, a knee-high wave pushes her to the ground. She lies still in the soggy sand as the second wave crashes on top of her, covering her like a blanket. For a bleak moment, the ocean paralyses Eden. The crashing waves never seem to draw back from the beach as they keep coming in a uniform manner. Being under the cool salty sea makes Eden shiver. She feels Henry pulling her straight up to her feet.

"Are you all right?"

Eden looks at Henry in a daze, her vision blurred. Beyond him, she notices grey clouds on the horizon that seem to have appeared out of nowhere. The gale wind blows her partially dry. Eden turns stiffly around in time to see the final tree in the sunny spotlight. She rapidly blinks her eyes to eliminate the blurriness. An Edwardian-style house appears in front of the sun, beaming through a tree, like an apparition. As quickly as the flashing vision appears, it disappears. Eden turns back around to Henry.

"I'm fine."

Suddenly, the wind dies. Henry helps Eden into the lifeboat while battling with the banging waves. He quickly hops into the boat. The lifeboat begins to jolt as the rattling ropes move. Eden sits and shivers vigorously. Henry reaches out and gently grabs her hand from her lap. She looks up and smiles. Even with the warm comfort, she continues to shiver. They sit in silence for the remainder of the jittery ascent.

The lifeboat halts parallel to the *Marida*'s boat deck. Henry hops out and helps Eden out. Captain Ainsley and Louis are standing on the boat deck. Henry and Eden immediately approach them.

"Eden, are you OK? You appear to be cold and wet," Captain Ainsley asks.

"I'm fine, Father. I just wasn't expecting the water to be so lively."

Torrential rain pelts down. The chattering crowds on the bow and boat deck scurry about like ants as they simultaneously enter the indoor sections of the *Marida*. Captain Ainsley, Louis, Henry, and Eden all seek shelter in the bridge. The rain is so heavy that the island is now barely visible. Eden stares out to the island, not so much to see the island, which can't be seen, but so she can better understand the vision she saw earlier.

"What now, Captain?" Henry asks.

"We now wait for two ships; one is a large passenger liner big enough to accommodate an extra sixteen hundred souls, and the other vessel will tow the *Marida* back to Belfast."

"OK, in the meantime, I better get Eden changed into something a little dryer," Henry says.

Eden can barely hear the men's conversation from a few feet away due to the heavy rainfall.

"By the way, what was your evaluation on the *Marida*'s status?" Louis asks.

"She's a little banged up due to colliding head-on into a boulder the size of a tugboat, but other than that, I reckon she's right for the sea."

"That would explain the impact of last night's crash," Captain Ainsley says.

Eden breaks eye contact with the island and turns around in time to see Henry approach her. Gradually, the rain eases. She feels her skin tightening with goosebumps. Her damp hair hangs down to her shoulders. Henry takes off his jacket and drapes it across Eden.

"We can go to your cabin when you are ready."

"Yes, I was just admiring the island, even though I can barely see it." Eden turns to the landmass. "I'm imagining a little house just beyond the shoreline. I suppose I am just thinking how lovely it would be to live somewhere like this, maybe even raise a family." Eden turns to Henry. "However, I could never move from Ireland."

"It is your home, and that's where your family is."

The rain continues moderately. The mist thins a little, making the island barely visible.

"I am ready now." Eden turns and begins to make her way to the exit.

Henry follows. On the deck, just outside the bridge, Eden stops to glance out at the horizon. The drifting clouds allow the morning sun to beam its warmth. The rain eases to a drizzle, shimmering in the sunlight. As the weather begins to lift, so too do Eden's spirits.

She is more attentive to nature after her ordeal, she thinks as she continues along the deck with a smile.

May 10, 1911, 17:00

Nearing the end of the day brings the end of an adventurous journey. The mishap of boarding another ship in the midst of the voyage does not cause much delay. The destination afar appears to be nothing more than a shadowy outline upon the dimming horizon. I can feel the ship beginning to slow down. The approaching Statue of Liberty quickly vanishes behind the other side of the ship. A few ships sail about in the harbour, beautifully breaking the water. Little tugboats sail our way. The distant port draws closer, at a snail's pace. My excitement and nervousness heighten as the towering landscape now comes into focus. Welcome to New York City.

June 7, 1911, 18:20

The past month has gone by quickly. The land of opportunity really has a lot to offer. The luxurious hotel, fine dining, and entertainment from Broadway shows have been grand, but this has made me realise the ocean is where I truly belong. The deck of a ship, watching the sea, is the most serene place in the world. My father is about to command the RMS Mystic and sail us to Liverpool. I am excited to get on the open sea and sail back home to Europe.

July 18, 1913, 08.00

Sorry, journal, it has been two years since I have written anything, though I am hopeful there will be something worth writing about in the near future. Even though I expressed my love for the sea, I have spent these past two years preoccupied in Queenstown. A little while ago, our neighbour, Mrs Insen, fell ill. I have been working as a maid for the Insen family, helping with the cooking and cleaning and caring for their six beautiful children. Mrs Insen's condition is greatly improving, so my services are not needed as much. This is only unfortunate, seeing that I have grown to love cooking, cleaning, and childcare. I am also discovering a passion. Beyond writing entries in a journal, I dream to excel in creative writing. My first piece is a poem about a koala. Finding a picture in a textbook of this cute Australian marsupial perched in a tree was somewhat inspiring. The next piece I am thinking about writing is a short story. Perhaps my inspiration *shall come when I finally travel across the open sea once again. Though I feel ready to settle down and become a wife and mother, the ocean, my first love, still calls to me. Another voyage has been in the back of my mind ever since I stepped off the RMS Mystic at the Queenstown Port. However, other lovely things have come forward. It is the love that would make my whole world complete. Even after two years, I believe fate will have it that I will be with Henry Delighkan.*

Early morning fog covers the Irish city of Belfast, making it barely visible from the harbour. The sun is a dim glow just above the horizon. Henry, wearing his typical tie, vest, and button coat, stands on the bow of the *Marida*. Three men approach him. They slightly resemble Henry in their physical characteristics, but not in their manner of dress code, as they wear pants with suspenders and a simple button top. Henry gives the still invisible landscape of Belfast one last gaze before facing his older brothers, Fredrick, George, and Samuel.

"I never get tired of admiring the ships we help build," Fredrick says in his Irish accent.

"Yes, this ship is worthy of admiring. What are you all doing now?"

"Same as you at the moment, looking out at our hometown before we set sail," George says.

"We're actually finishing loading the last of the cargo. Father wants you on the dock," Samuel says.

A youthful-looking lady wearing a simple yet elegant long, flowing dress with a broad matching hat approaches the men. Meredith smiles while looking towards the foggy city.

"Sorry, Mother. We will resume preparing the ship now," Henry says.

"I know my sons are hard workers, so they do deserve a brief break to look out at their hometown."

"As nice as the landscape is, I had better get back to work—with George and Samuel's assistance, of course."

Nodding in agreement, George and Samuel begin walking off with Fredrick following.

"No need to apologise. If anything, I need to thank you. I am greatly looking forward to your father's retirement once this final project is complete. You are definitely living up to the Delighkan name, considering the brilliant ideas and designs you have had with this project, which we all shall soon call home."

The comment boosts Henry's self-esteem.

"I can always count on your positivity. I better go and see Father on the dock."

He walks along the bow's deck until he reaches a little gate. Passing through the little gate and down a short, steep stairwell, he walks through a white metallic door. He makes his way along the narrow corridor. At a "T" intersection, he continues down yet another narrow corridor. Opening a metallic door, Henry is now in a wider, more decorative corridor, with fancy light fixtures on the walls and along the carpet runner. This corridor leads him to the D-deck level of the stairwell, which appears similar to the upper-level stairwell. Passing under an archway and continuing a couple of paces along the wide, decorative corridor, he finally reaches the gangplank protruding from the *Marida*'s open entrance door.

Edward Delighkan, carrying middle-aged plumpness under his vest and tie and scratching at his curly moustache, stands at the base of the gangplank. As Henry approaches his father, an automobile pulls up about ten feet away. The automobile appears like a metallic carriage, with a black canopy and a floating steering wheel behind a narrow pane of glass. Martin hops out from the driver's seat and helps his wife, Stella, out from the passenger's side. Eden and his younger daughter, Evelyn, help themselves out from towards the rear of the automobile. All three ladies are casual yet elegant, with broad hats to match their garments. Martin's suit somewhat resembles Henry's fashion. The Ainsleys approach the Delighkans.

"Top of the morning, Ainsley family," Henry says.

"Good morning, Henry," Martin says.

"This is my father, Edward."

"It's a pleasure to finally meet you. I admire your work, sir," Martin shakes Edward's hand.

"Thank you. As do I, your expansive commanding career is pretty impressive."

"Thanks for the compliment. This is my wife, Stella, and my two daughters, Eden and Evelyn."

"How do you do, I am sure you ladies would like to find your staterooms. With Henry telling me how much Eden loves this ship, it would be a pleasure if she leads the way. We gentlemen need to discuss something before we board."

Henry hides his nervousness with a smile.

"It would be a pleasure, sir."

Henry's eyes follow Eden as she steps up the narrow gangplank. Her mother and sister follow. Now the ladies are out of sight, he calms a little and ensures himself there's nothing to be nervous about. It's only a life-changing moment greatly upon him. Henry turns his attention back to Martin and Edward.

"So, Edward, the wireless message was quite vague, care to elaborate?"

"Firstly, I apologise for getting you to come so early, seeing you had to come from Queenstown. The reason for you coming so early is this is not a typical passenger voyage leaving at noon. We're all that's aboard the *Marida* and we're going somewhere quite different to the destinations you've ever seen. Secondly, you're aware 'Blue Ocean Line' dissolved last year due to the *Marida*'s sister ship, the *Neris*. We now own the *Marida* and the scrapped parts of the *Neris* and we followed through with a brilliant destination Henry created. I know you're not far from retirement, but, I would like to offer you a job for the remaining of your impressive career."

"I suppose the job is just commanding the *Marida* by sounds of it to one place, then back again. That'll be a great way to ease into retirement."

"That's basically it."

"Yes, I will take you up on your offer."

Henry confidently gains his courage.

"I would also like to propose something."

CHAPTER 5

July 23, 1913, 06:00

This voyage on the Marida is a mystery to me.

The florescent full moon hangs low in the pale blue and pink sky. The *Marida* breaks water as she steams gracefully along. Eden leans back in a deck chair. Her thin white nightgown drapes on the boat deck, and her bare toes are free to wiggle. The still air has a hint of warmth. She stares up at the gradual illuminating sky as the new day shoos away the night's darkness. The scenery clears her mind. Creaking footsteps startle Eden, and she bolts upright to find Henry there.

"Eden, I wouldn't expect to see you roaming about this time of morning."

She's glad and at ease that the man to stumble upon her would be Henry.

"I felt quite warm in my cabin. I thought it would be lovely out here on deck."

"Are you comfortable now, or do you need me to do anything for you?"

"You are a kind and caring man. I'm fine, thank you."

"I hear you're quite caring yourself, with the way you helped your neighbours."

"It was a pleasure. I enjoyed cooking, cleaning, and tending to the children. My parents hired Molly some time ago to be my personal maid as my condition to sail. I often help Molly about the house, and I must say, we make a good team."

The graceful sun begins to peak. Eden stares at the calm horizon, about a kilometre away from the breaching sun. The orange glow warms her as it beams against the *Marida*.

"I could stare at this view forever," she says, her eyes fixed upon the horizon.

Suddenly, the sunlight disappears, as though something is obstructing the sun. The *Marida*'s speed noticeably decreases. The ship is inching closer to the thing blocking the sun, which is now beginning to rise above it. Thanks to the rising sun, it's clear now. The thing is an island. With confusion as to why the *Marida* would be approaching a tropical island seemingly in the middle of nowhere, Eden turns to Henry. He's kneeling down on one knee and holding a silver band diamond ring with both hands. She gasps.

"Eden Ainsley, will you call this island home and stare at the view forever with me?"

Her joyous emotions flood her eyes.

"Yes," she says under a whimper.

Henry rises to his feet and leans to kiss his to-be wife. Eden gives her heart to him, as she blindly gets lost in the moment.

She stands and turns to the horizon. The island is now close enough to see glimpses of the destination that's ahead, and yet they can remain on the open sea. The six-hundred-foot-long wooden dock extends along the sandy beach. There's a clearing amongst the flourishing forest. A massive six-storey building in this clear area catches their immediate attention. About half a dozen buildings about half the size sits not too far from the massive building. A Ferris wheel accompanies the bordering trees on the left side. Early-morning lights up the serene paradise. Eden lights with excitement as her extending smile indicates. Her smile, however, shrinks a little when she realises something.

"Is this the same island the *Marida* was marooned on two years ago during that big storm?"

"It sure is. Welcome to Suntree Bay."

August 29, 1913, 20.45

I am so excited while a wee bit nervous. Just about everything is ready, with less than a week until the most delightful day. My family seems to be settling well in their new parlour suit homes in the hotel. Mother and I have been helping cook in the hotel's kitchen, making beds and doing other little jobs to get the hotel rooms ready for guests. Even though there are servants to carry out these duties, I find my mother and I quite enjoy being hands-on. Watching Father leaving port days ago, it is still awing every time. This is the happiest I have ever seen my father. The idea of commanding the Marida to and from this beautiful paradise must be doing wonders for him. Evelyn and I love the view from our hotel room's balcony. With the entire ocean not far, it is as if we are on the deck of the Marida. Between the placid sea during the day and the starry sky at night, as well as the forest of beautiful trees meeting the changing skies, this place is a true treasure. Sharing it with Evelyn is the ultimate delight. I cannot wait for the moment I say to guests, "Welcome to Suntree Bay," as Henry said to me.

September 3, 1913, 07.00

The big day is finally here. The day Henry and I say " I do." The day the Marida arrives at port with more than just Delighkans and Ainsleys aboard. The day I become Eden May Delighkan.

The blinding midday sun beams down on Eden. Not a single cloud interrupts the bright blue sky. She sits on a wooden park bench under a thirty-foot-tall gum tree. This tree, which lacks the foliage to be completely sheltering, is the centrepiece of the town garden. The town garden is a large grassy area meeting to the street's footpath and the street barriers this area in a square formation. The footpath linking the gum tree to the street is blooming with flowers and small shrubs. The street's footpath also blooms with flowers and shrubs, creating a peaceful border for the grassy area.

Circling the town garden from the other side of the street are buildings. The building lining up to the gum tree's footpath is a massive six-storey grand hotel that's as wide as it is tall. It's white with golden borders around the windows and decorative carvings looking like leafy vines going up the walls. The revolving door is welcoming under an arching marquee. The street continues straight past the hotel with a sign saying "Pool, Tennis Court, Gymnasium" on the right-hand side.

Adjacent to the hotel is the theatre. This building is about half the size with two thick columns with four steps in between and a red carpet that flows inside the building past glass double doors. Next to the theatre is the library. Standing at three storeys, it's half the size of the hotel but is identical, with its golden borders, carvings, and arch marquee. The only difference is directly above the marquee on top of the building, there's a huge Roman numeral clock with its own tiny roof. Beside the library is the restaurant. This large-level building has a complete glass front that gives a glimpse of a few tables set up with a white tablecloth, shiny cutlery, triangular napkins, and a small flowering shrub as the centrepiece.

Adjacent to the restaurant is a carousel. The ready to go round horses and the carnival appealing design would surely bring smiles to children's faces. On the right of the carousel, a street extends with a sign beside it saying, "Ferris wheel and hospital bay." To the left of the carousel is the town hall. This two-storey building is stone white with two thick columns and four steps leading to a single heavy glass door. Like the hotel, there's a blooming footpath lining up from the town hall to the gum tree. Lastly, to complete the third side of the square surrounding the town garden is an alfresco cafe. This outside dining has an open view to the vast ocean. There's a small counter in the back corner and a huge wooden lattice stretching from floor to ceiling to conceal the neighbouring town hall. Eight tiny square tables accompany four wicker chairs, each of which remains perfectly bare. The top half of the Ferris wheel towers from behind the town hall and alfresco cafe. A cool breeze gently knocks the Ferris wheel's little carriages.

Eden swings around and looks up at the library to confirm the time is a little after noon. She then faces forward and looks out at the calm ocean. The six-hundred-foot wooden dock is bare, with only two tugboats beside it. Evelyn approaches the park bench and sits beside Eden.

"Seeing that you weren't in the hotel, I thought I would find you here."

"Henry sent a telegram message saying to meet him here when the *Marida* arrives at port, which should be any moment now."

"This is a lovely spot for a man to greet his lovely fiancée after a voyage, but shouldn't you be getting ready for your big day?"

"The grand opening of Suntree Bay and sharing this place and Henry and my special moment with family and the *Marida*'s voyagers is what makes today a big day. Everything else is just in the details. I haven't forgotten my roots, though. Sometimes I think of Ireland and somewhat wish to be there, but I see Suntree Bay as a new chapter that I'm keen to fulfil and see what happens next."

"I feel much the same about Ireland while also loving the beauty of Suntree Bay. You're such an adventurous and free-spirited person, Eden. I wish I could be more like that, perhaps like when you were on the maiden voyage of the *Marida* two years ago. When you recount the voyage it sounded like quite an adventure, and I would have seen Suntree Bay sooner."

"You were tending to Mother at the time. I should have cared for Mother while she was ill, seeing how much I loved caring for the Insen family. But the opportunity to sail came about, and you can't be two places at once."

"Between me and the servants and maids, Mother was well taken care of."

"My near drowning bringing about an apparition of a house was seemingly significant, though it's an adventure I would not want to repeat."

Evelyn's eyes widen, and her bottom jaw drops a little. Eden looks at her sister's expression, remembering that only Henry knows of the drowning incident. The bellowing sound of a whistle blowing attracts the attention of the sisters. They look out at the horizon to see the *Marida* a couple of metres away from the dock. The two little tugboats steam towards the halting ship. The sisters continue to watch from afar as the little boats tether themselves to the large vessel, and then, tugging it along until the *Marida* is in the berthing position alongside the dock.

Eden sits patiently yet eagerly. The *Marida* sounds off another bellowing whistle. Eden stands and walks along the footpath until she reaches the street. Evelyn remains on the park bench. She looks down at the continuing street, which eventually meets with the dock three kilometres away. Meredith exits the hotel. Eden only has to step a couple of paces in order to talk to Meredith.

"It's a fine day, Mrs. Delighkan, isn't it?"

"Very pleasant indeed, and you are a true treasure worthy of a perfect day. I couldn't be happier for you and Henry."

"Thank you for making me feel welcome." Eden smiles. "Anyway, I better get back to my sister. I just wandered over here for a better view."

"Very well, carry on."

Eden backtracks along the footpath. She returns to the park bench but remains standing. A young couple with entwining arms walk along the street and towards the hotel. They're wearing the typical suit and long dress and both wearing hats to match their outfits. Eden admires from a distance as the couple appear to resemble her and Henry—young, happy, and close. It isn't long before more people are walking along the street. They mostly stay within the vicinity of the hotel, with the odd few wandering about. The young couple dawdles about halfway up the footpath leading to the gum tree.

"Hello, and welcome to Suntree Bay," Eden catches their attention.

They walk to the end of the footpath.

"Hello, are you Eden?" the woman asks.

"Yes, I am."

"Henry often spoke of you as we dined with him. He said you were somewhat his inspiration for Suntree Bay."

"I'm sure he was just being modest."

"Anyway, it appears we made the right choice for our honeymoon. This island is simply breathtaking."

"I hope you enjoy your stay and don't hesitate to ask if you need anything."

"Thank you. Well then, we better continue on our way."

Eden smiles as the honeymooning couple walk away. A crowd of hundreds of people seemingly continues to grow within the town garden area. Evelyn rises and stands beside Eden.

"This is quite the turnout."

"Yes, I see why Henry wanted to meet me in a specific spot." Eden looks intensely at the growing crowd.

Henry pops out from the crowd and approaches the sisters. He's carrying something big, requiring both hands, but Eden can't tell what it is due to a light throw-over blanket, concealing it. Henry places it on the vacant park bench. Eden looks down at the mysterious item and then quickly returns her attention to Henry.

"I wanted to give you a little gift and thanks to Evelyn's help. I know you're going to love it." Henry pulls away the blanket.

Eden looks down to find a blue budgie bird in a golden cage. She gives Henry a tight hug and then hugs Evelyn while holding a joyous smile.

"Thank you so very much. I just feel bad because I admit I haven't got a gift for you."

"You gave me a great gift a little while ago, which was an inspiration."

The bird begins to happily chirp. Eden sits beside the cage and singles out the song of the bird, as though she and the bird are in their own soundproof bubble.

"So what do you think you are going to call your little buddy?" Evelyn asks.

Evelyn's question doesn't seem to faze Eden much as she continues to admire her new little friend.

The low-hanging afternoon sun peeps through the hotel lobby's revolving door. Eden stands by the concierge desk, feeling the intensity of nervousness through her heart near beating out of her chest and heating fluster. She's wearing a long white dress with diamond sequences on her corset pushing chest and exposing arms as the sleeves go about halfway down the upper arm. Her curly hair is down, with a flower clip pulling the hair away from her left ear. As she slips on her white gloves, her father, who looks like his straight from the *Marida*'s bridge, approaches her.

"Even going with a simple wedding, you still look stunningly beautiful."

"Thank you, Father. Henry and I sharing our love and our island home with the world is all that matters to me today."

"Very well. Are you ready to go and share?"

Eden holds her arm out ready for her escort. She picks up a sunflower from the concierge desk with her other hand. Martin escorts her to the revolving doors. They individually glide through and then join again once outside. It doesn't appear as though a wedding is about to take place because the town garden looks the same as it did at midday. People mingle throughout the town garden area. They're all wearing formal garments, as if they're ready for a fancy dinner party. Eden immediately sees Henry presenting smartly in a tuxedo as he stands under the gum tree. Seeing him scares all her bad nerves away. Her family and his family are close by. A middle-aged half-bald celebrant stands beside Henry.

The library's clock tower bells ring, striking five o'clock. The whole town garden falls silent. Martin continues to escort his daughter along the footpath and stops at Henry. He smiles at both Henry and Eden, gives Eden a quick hug and then joins Stella and Evelyn nearby. Henry's parents and brothers stand beside the Ainsleys. Everyone's attention now belongs to Henry and Eden. The setting sun glows upon the island like a candle. Eden gives a glimpse at the sunset before returning to Henry. It's as though Henry and Eden are the only two people in the world as she deeply stares into his warm eyes.

"Eden you are the light in my life. You're the reason why I call Suntree Bay home—because you're the soul of this place. The greatest adventure I could ever imagine is spending the rest of my life with you. I will always love and cherish you and keep you forever in my heart."

"I believe fate gave me the desire to sail. Being on the *Marida*'s boat deck that day brought me to you and from that moment you have given me the comfort feeling that everything is OK. I trust you with my heart, and I'm ready to share my life with you. So long as you are forever by my side, I can always call Suntree Bay home."

The celebrant steps aside to reveal the blue budgie on the park bench. In front of the cage, there's a small silk pillow nursing two golden wedding bands. Eden places her sunflower beside the cage. Henry and Eden pick up the rings and slip them onto each other's finger. They hold hands while staring at each other dazedly. The celebrant steps back beside Henry and Eden.

"Do you Henry take, Eden Ainsley, to be your wife?"

"I do."

"Do you Eden take, Henry Delighkan, to be your husband?"

"I do."

"I now pronounce you husband and wife."

Henry and Eden lean forward and kiss, forever sealing their love. Applause breaks the silence. After Mr. and Mrs. Delighkan's kiss, the surrounding crowd quietens.

"My wife and I would like to welcome all of you to delightful Suntree Bay, and we hope you all have a pleasant evening. Thank you so much for being part of the grand opening to our island home and the beginning of the rest of our lives. Enjoy the celebration, and enjoy your stay on Suntree Bay."

An orchestra band sets up on the street in front of the hotel. They begin playing upbeat dinner party music. Waiters in white tuxedos come out from the restaurant carrying silver trays. Some obtain full champagne flutes, while others obtain hors d'oeuvres. Eden watches on as people help themselves to the waiter's offerings and feel the rhythm of the music. Seeing everyone enforcing the happy atmosphere fills her with overwhelming joy. Her parents swaying together in a slow pace dance nearby makes Eden smile in awe.

"That will be us one day." Eden gazes at Henry.

Henry looks at the long-lasting affectionate Ainsleys and then turns to Eden.

"I would like to show you something now."

Henry escorts Eden. They walk to a street beside the hotel that intersects with the dock's street. Henry's automobile, which looks identical to the Ainsley family's automobile, is waiting on the curb.

"We can't leave now. It would be rude toward our guests," Eden says.

"Don't worry. It will be quick, and then we'll come straight back."

They hop in the automobile. Henry starts the engine and drives off. The calm ocean is an easy view from the straight road. The dimming sun appears to be trailing them as it pokes through the odd few trees that border the road. After about five kilometres of travel, Henry turns the automobile onto a smooth lengthy driveway and continues along until he reaches an Edwardian house. They hop out of the automobile. Eden stares at the house in awe. The twin thin white columns supporting an arching awning above a small square doorstep is a welcoming appeal. The two-storey house isn't a cube shape; rather, to the right of the front door, it's as though there's a segment missing with this wall beginning about halfway down. Four huge windows with decorative white borders cover the front view. A blooming flower bed sits underneath the ground window to the left of the shiny oak front door.

"It's beautiful."

"It's our new home." Henry walks to the front door and opens it.

Eden follows him with excitement like a child on Christmas morning. The remaining ounce of daylight left faintly pours in through the huge windows. The hollow foyer smells of fresh paint and wood. The slightly curved wood staircase in the centre of the area catches immediate attention. Eden unnoticeably slips on the glossy wooden floor as she impatiently enters the house. Henry enters the house and stands beside Eden by the banister.

"So do you like the house?"

Eden presses tightly against his body as she wraps her arms around his lower back and then kisses him.

"Annabelle."

She looks up from the journal and scans the chilly, dim room.

"Wanda?" Annabelle asks the seemingly empty room while placing the journal on the desk.

A sudden gust of wind blows the stiff air and flutters a couple of loose papers off the desk. A faint outline of a person stands beside a nearby bookcase. There are no physical characteristics of this person. Rather, it appears like a foggy body.

"Eden?" Annabelle questions as she quints.

Before Annabelle has the chance to confirm, the figure disappears. She stands and curiously walks over to the bookcase. Catching her attention, she pulls a thick, hardcover photo album off the shelf, walks back towards the desk, and sits down. The lantern is all but a faint glow. The first photograph is a black and white shot of Henry and Eden under the gum tree on their wedding day. Flipping through the photo album, there's Henry and Eden on the banister in their house, on the beach, and standing alongside immediate family members with various locations of Suntree Bay as backdrops. Then, there's Eden rubbing a baby bump.

Baby photos become kid photos as they grow throughout the 1920s. A family portrait of the Delighkans standing in front of the family home consists of Henry and Eden with their four children, ranging from a five-year-old to a twelve-year-old. Reaching the last page of the album, Annabelle closes it and puts it back in the shelf. As she does so, the neighbouring book catches her attention. It's an A4 size hardcover book with a bit of paper poking out from the top, which reads "Time Travel." She pulls out this book, walks back to the desk, and sits down.

On the first page, there's a drawing of a steam tugboat.

I, Henry Delighkan, have the idea for time travel. The time machine is a steam tugboat, more precisely, my first ever design project as an apprentice. To my theory there are two requiring elements for time travel, speed and energy. With my calculation, the boat needs to travel at least twenty-five knots to gain the speed. The energy is achievable by using a metal conductor as the coal burns in the furnace. With the right technique, this should create immense energy. This experiment will take place in the depths of the Suntree Bay forest.

Annabelle stretches her stiff neck by rolling her head like a ball. As she does this, she glances out a huge nearby window to see daylight beginning to break. She closes up the book and plonks it on the desk. Seeing the natural light coming into the room, she blows out the dimming glow from the lantern.

"Time travel would be the definite answer to the mystery, provided that it's more than just a theory. Something worth scoping out," she says loudly and excitedly, like a scientist with a theory.

She hops off the chair, leaves the office, and walks towards the front door. Using quick motions, she picks up her handbag from beside the front door and locks the door on her way out as she forms a smirk. Being optimistic about time travelling has put her in a good mood. After strolling off the doorstep, Annabelle taps the side of the hood of her car twice as she decides to continue her journey on foot.

The smooth, lengthy driveway seems to have the slightest decline, which is not noticeable when travelling by car. The fresh morning air barely touches nearby trees. Annabelle looks at her watch when reaching the end of the driveway. The time is a little after six o'clock. A car would often drive by probably the early morning workers heading to their jobs. The morning sun begins to peek out from behind the faraway houses. She continues along Grand Ocean Road. Traffic keeps to a steady flow. The ocean is calm with only small waves breaking ashore. The serene view clears Annabelle's mind as she walks along in her natural quick pace.

After about five kilometres of walking along the same road she reaches the town while maintaining her pace. Passing the hotel, she halts in her travels. The shady air is cool. The touch of a lonely ray of sunlight is warm. She pushes through the revolving doors.

The foyer is quiet. An elderly couple of about ninety years old approaches Annabelle. The man slightly hunches as he leans on his wooden cane. The woman, seemingly fit for her age, stands straight with no aid.

"Good morning, sir, ma'am. Anything the matter?"

"Nothing is wrong. I was just wondering, are you related to Henry and Eden Delighkan?" the man asks.

"Yes, I'm Annabelle Delighkan."

"My parents were honeymooners at the grand opening and would later move to this island. My husband and I attended Henry and Eden's eightieth wedding anniversary aboard the *Marida*. That was a fun night until Henry and Eden were just simply gone," the woman says.

"I'm honoured to meet someone who was born and raised here and after many years still calls Suntree Bay home."

"I feel much the same meeting a Delighkan. Anyway, we better get going."

"Yes, our great-grandson and his fiancé are expecting us. They're here for the centenary anniversary," the man says.

"I better get going myself. Take care now," Annabelle excuses herself.

Annabelle walks a few paces to the left and enters a spacious room through a huge archway. This room appears similar to a public room aboard the *Marida*, with decorative carvings in the walls and ceiling beams. Two green button lounges with curving wooden legs face each other in the middle of the room. Pot plants in the corners grow tall. The stone column fireplace lays dormant in the middle of the adjacent wall. Early morning is now really hitting its peak as daylight streams in through the three windows that make up the wall on the opposite side of the room. Annabelle strolls in and immediately approaches the fireplace. She firstly admires the huge painting hanging above the fireplace. It's a painting of the island of Suntree Bay with the *Marida* beside it. The turquoise ocean and the clear bright sky capture the essence of a tropical paradise. Next to lure Annabelle is what appears to be a fairy wand—a green stick looking like a flower stem with a glittering silver star. Looking at the wand makes her reminisce about sleepovers at her great grandparent's house as a child. Grandma Eden would often read "Charley Star," her own story about a bird and a fairy having adventures around the world. Grandpa Henry had this wand made to recognise Eden's creativity.

Annabelle picks up the wand. "This would be grand as a metal conductor, provided that it's actually made of metal."

She shivers as though there's a sudden ten-degree temperature drop. She dawdles over to the window to catch the warm sunlight dribbling in. A ding sound comes from her handbag, so she pulls out her phone. It's a text message from her mother just, simply saying, "Homebound." The chill remains in the air. If anything, it feels even colder. Annabelle places her handbag and the wand on the nearby lounge and swiftly replies to the text:"When do you think you'll arrive at port?" She sits on the lounge, waiting for a reply with her phone in her hand. Her phone dings shortly after. The text reads, "Here."

Annabelle springs to her feet and rushes to a smaller window that's adjacent to the entrance, throwing her phone on the lounge in the process. She peers out the window hoping to find out if the ferry is at port. There's a clear view of the town garden; however, the marina can't be seen at all from this window's perspective. A reflection of a transparent humanly figure suddenly appears in the window. Annabelle quickly spins around to find no one there. She begins to breathe deep and fast, swearing to herself that the reflection was of a ghost. In the middle of her hyperventilating, she feels something hard and forceful striking the left side of her forehead. In a blurry daze, she drops to the floor. What hit her? The more puzzling question: how did her phone end up on the floor beside her? She intensely blinks a couple of times to adjust her eyesight. Sitting up very slowly, she reaches for her phone and presses the home button. The device doesn't respond. A tiny red dot on the side of the phone catches Annabelle's attention. She squints intensely.

"Annabelle."

Hearing her name makes her jump as she then looks up. The elderly lady from the foyer stands with a concerning look.

"Are you all right?"

"Uh, yes, I'm fine." Annabelle stands with a slight wobble. "Hey, um, am I bleeding at all?"

"No, are you sure you're all right?"

"Thanks for the concern. I am fine, really." Annabelle shoves her phone in her bag, picks up the bag and the fairy wand. "Bye." She leaves the room.

Annabelle exits the hotel. On the street, she looks out towards the ocean to confirm the ferry is indeed at port. The clock tower's bells begin to chime as the clock strikes seven o'clock. She glances at her watch and realises it's frozen at six forty-five. Shrugging it off, she continues her travels along the street.

By now the illuminating sun shines freely in the open sky. The odd car putters by. Annabelle passes a flat building with "Sports Centre" written on a big marquee. A huge tennis court neighbours this building. Walking and walking along with the same stride, she continues on past a four-way intersection. Farther on, there's a massive grassy field which separates the high school from the road. Continuing on for another kilometre or so, she steps over the railway track as she reaches the boundary of the town. She enters the luscious forest.

The air is still. Sunlight faintly streams through the thick growing canopy. Sound is scarce. A soft giggle, sounding like a little girl, has Annabelle curiously stopping and listening. Not hearing a thing in a brief moment of silence, she continues on slowly. A blue budgie bird flies in and lands on a low branch close to Annabelle's general direction.

"Hello, Charley," Annabelle jokes as she passes the bird.

"Hello, Annabelle."

Hearing the voice that seems to have come from directly behind her, she shoots her head around to find nothing. Even the budgie is no longer there. An odd idea plays through Annabelle's mind as she treks on the crunchy leafy forest floor. Eden's characters, Charley and Star, are real. A separating beam of sunlight streams through the crowd of trees. The sun welcomes the early morning's singing birds. The trickling sound of moving water becomes more prominent as she slowly ventures on. Pulling down a massive low growing leaf, she reveals what she's looking for. This large stream runs through the forest and meets the ocean at both ends, basically sectioning Suntree Bay into two islands. Annabelle knows this body of water's flow because she and Wanda would often explore through the forest as kids. No moment of stopping, she treks alongside the muddy bank.

The gently flowing stream momentarily clears Annabelle's busy mind.

About two kilometres downstream, she finds it. Henry's tugboat gently rocks as a thick rope connects it to a nearby sturdy tree. It's a six-foot-long vessel, looking a little like a century-old fisherman's boat, with a lonely smokestack standing in the middle of the cabin's roof. Annabelle firstly approaches the anchoring tree and unties the dirty rope with great difficulty. After about a minute of intense weaving, the tugboat is free. She eagerly hops aboard and enters the cabin, immediately dropping her bag on the floor near the entrance. It's quite bright in here due to the many small windows along three walls. The helm stands in the centre and is accompanied by a golden telegraph. Annabelle looks at the contraptions with the daunting expression thinking, *How do I drive this thing?*

A nearby window fogs up, reading a message, "I'll lead you." An illustration of a star appears beside the message. There's no denying it now—Star seems to be very much real. Suddenly Annabelle feels lucid and calm, as though a person from 1913 with background experience in the shipping industry is possessing her. She opens a hatch to shovel in some coal in a burning bunker. Before closing the hatch, she throws the metallic wand on top of the pile of coal. She then pulls the lever on the telegraph and, lastly, casually grabs the helm.

Annabelle decides to wait until she reaches the open sea to increase speed. She feels easier this way because of her unfamiliar know-how of operating this vessel. The tugboat cruises along smoothly. The surrounding dense forest has an isolation appeal to it, forgetting that there's a town only kilometres away. Eden's journal and photo album comes to Annabelle's mind. She wonders about the short time between Henry and Eden's wedding to starting their family. The morning's daylight becomes brighter and the crowd of trees diminish. The tugboat approaches the end of the stream.

Entering the sea is like a breath of fresh air. The mid-morning sun beams down from the clear blue sky. The salty sea breeze is strong yet refreshing. Choppy waves bang against the tugboat's hull.

Annabelle opens the coal bunker's hatch and shovels in at least three piles of coal. She shuts the hatch and pulls on the telegraph's lever.

"Full steam ahead," she excitedly says under a big smile.

The tugboat clocks more and more speed while the choppy waves become increasingly violent. She tightens her grip on the helm. The rough sea throws around the seemingly weightless tugboat. Splashing waves drench Annabelle. Suddenly, the sea calms a little, just enough to give the tugboat a small path. The tugboat zooms by, becoming faster and faster. It reaches ultimate speed, almost flying along the water's surface. Something blocks the sun, making it appear overcast. Annabelle looks to the side and immediately gasps in fear. A massive tsunami-like wave towers over the little tugboat. She braces herself by tightening her grip on the helm, to the point where she begins to develop blisters. It feels like an eternity before the wave plummets. The crashing wave forcefully submerges her.

She can't see anything, but she can feel the powerful water throwing her and possibly debris from the tugboat hitting her. The strong sea holds her captive. It's forever before Annabelle finally breaches the surface. Another massive wave plummets down. She feels herself blindly whirling through the water. *Thump!* She hits the sandy shore hard.

Annabelle opens her eyes to find the beat-up tugboat only a couple of feet away from her. She slowly sits up and looks at the tugboat. The smokestack is gone, the windows are hollow and a few panels from the hull are missing. The fairy wand is somehow lying on the beach beside her. She picks it up as she wobbles to her feet. Her heavy head feels a little dizzy. Looking directly in front of her beyond the beach, as luck would have it, there's the Delighkan House. The whipping sea breeze causes her soaking body to shiver. Trembling, she shoves the tip of the wand in the back of her pants and conceals it under her wet shirt. With a stumble in her step, she slowly begins to walk towards the house.

CHAPTER 6

Annabelle dawdles along the dry squeaky sand. The high sun warms her a little. Her clothes stiffen as they slightly start to dry, thanks to the knocking sea breeze. The warmth from the sun and the calming walk help ease her fuzzy feeling from the sea incident.

"Well, that achieved absolutely nothing," she mumbles glumly.

Approaching the doorstep of the Delighkan House, Annabelle frantically pats herself down, suddenly realising the absence of her handbag. By chance, she twists the doorknob. To her surprise, the door opens. She definitely recalls locking it, so this is a mystery. Upon entering the house, things are noticeably different. The eerie chill is absent. The foyer is welcomingly fresh, as if someone has recently come through here with a duster. Henry and Eden step out of the lounge room. They look so happy and youthful and alive. Annabelle stares at them, her eyes watering.

"Can we help you miss?" Henry asks.

"No, I'm sorry for intruding. Sorry." Annabelle walks out the front door before her emotions have the chance to burst.

Seeing Henry and Eden alive and in the flesh overwhelms Annabelle as she wipes away the odd streaking tear. Briefly stopping in her travels, she notices the absence of her CR-V. There are enough clues to convince her that travelling through time has been a success. She's not entirely sure when, exactly. The success puts a smile on her face. She continues her travels down the smooth lengthy driveway. The Delighkan House is literally the only house. The land where the residential area is in the future is currently an extension of the surrounding dense forest. She heads along the adjoining Grand Ocean Road.

The beat-up tugboat on the beach is just visible from here. Not a single person or vehicle shares this road with Annabelle. She pushes her aching legs, a little overzealous in reaching the town garden. The glaring sun causes her to squint. Her clothing is mostly dry, except for the undercarriage areas. She breathes deep and heavy, thinking to herself, *Gee, I need to get into shape.* Travelling five kilometres on foot, she has arrived at her destination.

The garden surrounding the gum tree looks virtually the same now as it does in 2013, besides the shrubbery being a little undergrown. All the buildings look so new and fresh. It's as if Annabelle is seeing her old town in new light. She wanders along the street in front of the hotel. The clock tower's bell rings. It's officially midday.

People give Annabelle a blank stare as they walk by. Why is this? It could be because she's still partially wet with damp hair, looking like she's come directly from a swimming pool. More to the point, she doesn't match up with the fashion trends. Everyone's wearing long, elegant dresses with broad hats and classy suits with bowler hats. She thinks back to Henry and Eden; their attire is much the same, minus the hats.

The fashion gives Annabelle the rough idea that she's seeing Suntree Bay in its infancy, but she's not entirely sure of the exact year. She dawdles through the garden and towards the gum tree. Admiring the vibrant plants and observing nearby people, she suddenly feels an irritable stinging sensation on the left side of her forehead. She instinctively rubs at it while plonking herself on the wooden park bench. The stinging is persistent. She continues to rub even though it doesn't get her anywhere. Something suddenly perks her attention and helps her to ignore the irritant to a point. Henry walks along the street and enters the hotel. Annabelle springs to her feet, approaches the hotel, and enters.

There seems to be no changes at all to the foyer, Annabelle observes as she wanders towards the concierge desk. A few other people wander about. Annabelle spots Henry talking to an elderly man by the curvy staircase. She studies him, her great grandfather, as a young man.

"Can I help you, ma'am?"

She turns to her side to find the concierge—a young Irish man in a bowtie and suit, with his shiny black hair, sleeked back.

"I'm fine for the moment, thanks."

He gives her a smile while standing straight. There's a *Sunny Times* newspaper sitting on the concierge desk that catches Annabelle's attention. Her eyes zoom in to the date at the top of the page without taking any notice of the headlines. Today's date is the seventeenth of November, 1913.

"Hello, Mr. Delighkan," the concierge greets.

Keeping her head down, Annabelle looks out the corner of her eye to find Henry standing right there. She stares down at the newspaper, pretending to read it.

"Hello, Mr. Richards, any messages for me?"

"Certainly, this just came through this morning."

"Thank you," Henry steps away from the desk.

She looks up to find Henry reading from a small slip of paper. His face drops and his eyes swell with forming tears. Henry stuffs the paper in his jacket pocket. Annabelle approaches him.

"I'm sorry, I couldn't help but notice that you're upset."

"I'm fine. Someone I know just passed away." He blinks, and the tears stream down his face.

Annabelle hugs him. She breaks away, feeling inappropriate.

"I'm sorry. You don't even know me."

"It's OK. If my wife were here, she would have done the exact same thing. I must say, you seem to resemble my wife a little in the face."

"It must be just a coincidence."

"Anyway, thank you for the hug and concern, but I'm OK, really."

"OK, good day to you then." Annabelle walks off.

"Annabelle, please be OK."

She frantically swings her head because, swearing that the voice belongs to Wanda. *How can this be? There's just no way.* It's disorientating to hear Wanda's voice, and so Annabelle accidently trips over someone's bulky trunk. She immediately springs to her feet, pretending she didn't just trip over. This is regretful though, because it brings on light-headedness. She stands with a wobbly stance. The feeling only lasts for a brief moment, but it's long enough to catch Henry's attention.

"I saw what happened. Are you OK?"

"I'm OK, thanks."

"If you like I can escort you to your room," Mr. Richards offers.

"Well, I'm not actually booked into the hotel."

"It's OK, you can stay with me. It's the least I can do to make sure you are indeed fine," Henry says.

"That's very kind of you."

"Good day, Mr. Richards." Henry escorts Annabelle to the exit.

The weaving of arms is unusual to Annabelle because she comes from a time when this is uncommon. They break apart to push through the revolving doors. Now they stand on the street individually.

"Are you all right to walk? That's how I got here from my house is all."

"A walk in the fresh air would do me great, so let's go." Annabelle sets off.

Henry sets off after her. Around the corner from the hotel's entrance, they begin walking along Grand Ocean Road.

"I'm sorry, I haven't introduced myself. I'm Henry Delighkan."

"I'm Annabelle." She pauses to think of a surname. "Remal."

It seems like the walk really is doing her justice. Besides a nagging pressure, almost like a dull headache, she feels well. They walk along in silence. Annabelle peers out the corner of her eye to notice Henry is still upset. His eyes are glassy and his blank expression stares forward.

"So you're the guy who designed Suntree Bay. I love your work."

"I'm honoured that you admire my work."

Annabelle peers over again to notice his blank expression becomes a subtle smile.

"Dearly noted," she says with the tugboat time machine floating through her mind.

Seeing the prestige condition of Suntree Bay and meeting young Henry is enough proof to make Annabelle truly believe she's in the year 1913. To no surprise meeting, young Eden would be the last convincing proof that time travel exists. They continue to walk along in silence.

"Nearly there," Henry says.

After about a dozen steps or so, they reach the base of the smooth, lengthy driveway. Annabelle pushes her tiring legs on, becoming anxious to meet Eden. Henry lags a little but remains close enough for Annabelle to feel his presence behind her. She slows down to look at the empty space where her CR-V would be. Henry passes her and approaches the front doorstep. She follows him as he enters the house.

Annabelle walks through the front door and looks around, as if entering a new house for the first time. Eden steadily descends the staircase. Annabelle stares at her in awe. Looking closely at Eden, Annabelle indeed notices the striking resemblance. Basically seeing a mirror image of herself in Eden and being in the Delighkan House makes her feel comfortable and familiar with Henry and Eden. Even at this new age, they don't in the slightest feel like strangers.

"Hello there, ma'am," Eden greets as she reaches the last step.

"This is Annabelle. Annabelle, this is my wife, Eden."

"It is a pleasure," Eden says.

"Likewise." Annabelle rubs the left side of her forehead due to the persistence of her dull nagging headache.

"Are you all right?"

"Annabelle had a bit of an incident earlier, so I offered for her to come here. I couldn't leave without knowing she's OK."

"Perhaps we should show you to our guest bedroom so you have somewhere to rest."

"Thanks for that."

Popping up from seemingly nowhere, a young maid wearing a navy blue dress and white lace apron stands beside Annabelle.

"I'll show you, miss."

"This is Mollie. She knows exactly when to pop up. She'll take care of you if you need anything," Henry says.

"Right this way miss." Mollie steps up the stairs. Annabelle follows.

Eden watches her guest walking up the stairs, studying her. Annabelle's fashion sense is a little alienating to her, with long dark blue pants and a thin button top barely covering her arms. To complete the bizarre outfit, her soft-looking shoe covering her whole foot seems to be tightly in place by knotting ropes.

"There's something quite odd about our guest," Eden says.

"What do you mean?"

"Besides her fashion, the way she looked at me. It was almost as if she were staring at a ghost."

"I'm sorry for inviting her, but I couldn't just leave her alone in her predicament. And also, this happened at the time I received some bad news. If she is making you a bit uncomfortable, I can politely ask her to leave."

"No, it's fine. What's the bad news?"

Henry pulls out the slip of paper from his jacket pocket.

"Louis committed suicide," Henry says under a choking whimper.

Eden immediately hugs him. Her first thought is to empathise with Henry, and then she thinks of Louis, a man with the reputation to be loving and caring towards people and ships.

"Well, the *Marida* leaves port tomorrow. I had better get organised so we're in Queenstown in time for the funeral."

"We should pack right away. First, I'll check in on our guest."

They walk up the stairs. Henry goes right while Eden turns left. She continues along the hallway, which has the staircase's railing running along one side as this hall hangs above the foyer. Eden stands in the doorway while feeling a little unsure. Annabelle frantically sits up on the bed.

"Wanda." She nervously stares at the empty flower pattern chair sitting in the corner.

"Annabelle."

Jumpy, she twists around to find Eden in the doorway.

"I'm sorry to startle you. I was just checking in on you."

"I'm fine, thanks."

It's ensuring for Eden to hear the gradual calm in Annabelle's voice.

"Don't hesitate if you need anything," Eden walks away.

She walks back along the hallway and passes the staircase. Eden enters her bedroom. Two empty trunks lay open on the double-size bed.

"So how's our guest?" Henry begins placing his clothes in one of the trunks.

"She seems fine."

"Good to hear. After I'm done packing, I'm returning to town."

"How are you holding up? Are we still going to dinner tonight, or would you like to give it amiss?"

"It's OK. Focusing on getting ready to leave port and dinner tonight might help keep my mind occupied."

She notices her husband's worried expression as he places another set of clothes in his trunk.

"What's troubling you, dear?"

"The big *why* question. I don't understand why Louis would kill himself. He was one of the happiest and most optimistic people I've ever known. My only thought is it has something to do with Blue Ocean Line finishing last year. It's just absurd to think something that happened a year ago made Louis do this."

"Try not to dwell on this one question. Instead, remember his happy optimism."

"You always know what to say. At the moment I just sound like a blubbering mess."

"It's good to express your emotions." Eden looks at her empty trunk. "I had better get packing if we want to make it to Queenstown."

Annabelle sits on the edge of the bed and looks at the empty chair. She swears Wanda is here and sounds as if she's sitting in this chair, not so much physically but more like an invisible form with a disembodied voice. This is impossible like a pig-flying kind of impossible because Wanda is safe and sound in 2013. But how else would she explain hearing her sister's voice twice? Has travelling one hundred years to the past affected her somehow mentally? Not wanting to overthink these questions, she stands and leaves the room.

Annabelle dawdles along the hallway and then leans over the railing to view the foyer from a bird's eye view. Seeing the curving staircase and spacious wooden floor from here kind of makes her feel as though she's looking into a dollhouse. She stands upright and turns her attention to the two glass doors opposite the staircase. Judging by the glare, it looks like a bright, sunny day outside. Suddenly she feels something wet and sticky on the left side of her forehead. She wipes her finger along this substance and holds it in front of her to see what it is. It's fresh blood. She rushes into a nearby bathroom. Looking into a small white frame mirror hanging above the shiny porcelain basin, she sees nothing is there, no blood or a cut of any kind. Calming herself and forgetting about this strange occurrence, she leaves the bathroom.

Dawdling along the hallway, she continues down the stairs but stops more than halfway. Annabelle flashes back to when she saw the silhouetted hand on the railing. This gives her a bit of a chill just thinking about it. Thinking of this incident reminds her of the ghostly presence in the office at the time of reading the journal in there. The fresh and welcoming appeal makes it evident that there are no ghosts present. She then finds it intriguing to check out the current condition of the office. Stepping down, she reaches the base of the stairs and walks along the foyer.

Passing the staircase, she enters the office. The room appears much the same as it does in 2013, minus the dust. There's a blueprint of a ship hanging from the chalkboard. She finds it fascinating and honouring to know that her great grandfather's work is so grand and a turn of the century technological marvel. After staring at the blueprint for a brief moment, she pulls away and draws her attention to the desk. In the centre of the desk, with the odd few papers surrounding it, there's an A4 size hardcover book. Looking like the *Time Travel* book, she opens it to the first page. She finds the drawing of the tugboat.

"I see you're feeling better."

Annabelle looks up to find Eden standing in the entranceway.

"Uh, yes. Sorry, I'm a bit of a wanderer."

"It's OK. I'm a bit of a wanderer too. I'm sure Henry would be flattered you reading his book. I'm quite flattered myself because he was inspired to write his time travelling story after I wrote a story about a bird and fairy travelling the world and having adventures."

Annabelle suddenly feels doubtful when learning that the time travelling concept is nothing more than a story. Could this just be a dream and not actually a voyage through time? This could explain the forehead incident and why she hears Wanda. No, she doesn't want to believe this is the case. She stares at Eden with a tear forming in her eye. Whether this is a dream or reality, she feels happy to see Eden standing here in front of her.

"I would love for you to meet someone this way," Eden says.

Annabelle steps out from the desk and walks towards Eden. She rubs at her eye to conceal her solitary tear.

They leave the office and enter the lounge room on the opposite side of the foyer. The lounge room looks quite different as to how Annabelle remembers it. Two leafy pattern sofas face each other in the middle of the room. A rectangular oak coffee table sits in between. A high-back armchair sits in the corner. A little bushy tree grows from a ceramic pot along the wall not far from the armchair. There's a golden birdcage on a small table in front of the huge glary window. A blue budgie, looking like the one Annabelle recalls from the forest, perches contently.

"This is Charley."

"I take it this is the bird in your story."

"She sure is—the one and only."

Annabelle looks at Charley.

"Pardon me, ladies. Your gowns are ready for this evening."

Annabelle turns to find Mollie.

"What's happening this evening?"

"Henry and I are having dinner with our family, and we would like you to join us."

"If I'm not imposing."

"It will be our pleasure."

The clear starry night sky hangs above Suntree Bay. A gentle refreshing breeze lingers through the air. The *Marida* is a shadowy outline out on the distant watery horizon. Annabelle stands on the street, waiting for Henry and Eden to hop out of Henry's automobile, which sits parallel to the curb. Henry escorts the two ladies into the nearby restaurant.

All the tables are ready for dining with cutlery and fresh cloth napkins on top of clean white low-hanging tablecloths. Emerald glass stain light fixtures hang in rows along the shiny oak walls of the spacious room. The lighting that they beam in the room is dimmed. Annabelle observes the handful of people already in their seats. She studies the women in particular, the way they sit straight and forward in their chairs, erecting their dainty pinkie finger while drinking from a porcelain teacup; some have their napkins covering their whole lap. She already feels the part by wearing a long ocean-blue sequined dress belonging to Eden, which matches the dress code of the other ladies.

They reach a huge vacant table and Henry pulls out two leather chairs for Eden and Annabelle to sit side by side. He walks to the opposite side of the table to sit facing Eden directly. Familiar faces only from a photo album of two ladies and a gentleman approach the table.

"Annabelle these are my parents and sister, Martin, Stella, and Evelyn. Mother, Father, and Evelyn, this is Annabelle," Eden says.

Everyone greets one another. Evelyn places herself beside Eden with her parents seating beside her. Not long after, more familiar faces, a gentleman and lady, arrive at the table.

"These are my parents, Edward and Meredith. Mother and Father, this is Annabelle. She's a young lady who we've offered our hospitality to," Henry says.

Everyone greets the Delighkans as they sit beside Henry.

"You're such a kind, helping lad," Edward says.

"Thank you. It was the least I could do."

"I appreciate it," Annabelle says.

Secretly she's ecstatic she's taken care of by Henry and Eden and finds it truly overwhelming to be dining with her ancestors. Three young men, also familiar from a family photo album, come up to the table.

"Lastly, these are my brothers, Fredrick, George, and Samuel. Men, this is Annabelle."

The Delighkan brothers acquaint themselves with everyone. They sit in the last three remaining chairs.

"I'm happy for you to join us for dinner, and I must say, you have a striking resemblance. Are you a member of the Ainsley family?" Fredrick asks.

"My family is pure Scottish, so I don't think I'm related," Annabelle lies.

"I would like to start the evening by having a moment of silence for Louis Fisher," Henry says.

Everyone takes a moment of silence to honour the memory of Louis Fisher. Though Annabelle is sorry for the loss, she can't drown out the passing with good memories, presumably the thoughts of everyone else at the table.

"Well, Louis was a good man who saw greatness and potential in everyone and everything," Martin says.

"I couldn't agree more," Edward says.

A young waiter, ready to go with a short pencil and pad, approaches the table. He circles the table and asks people individually for their order. Annabelle's eyes wander as she sees at a neighbouring table an elderly couple taking their seats. She looks at the couple and thinks of the high probability of their long history together.

"Pardon me, ma'am. What would you like?"

She snaps out of her trance to find a waiter standing beside her with his pencil and pad, ready to take her order.

"I'll have today's special, thanks."

"Very well, ma'am." He scribbles on his pad before continuing his way around the table.

Before long, the waiter leaves the vicinity of the table. Henry stands and smiles at Eden. Everyone immediately looks at him.

"To brighten the mood for the evening, Eden and I have something delightful to share. We're going to be parents."

Everyone applauds and congratulates the expectant parents. Annabelle's cheerfulness suddenly shatters when she sees a man staring deep almost through her. His outfit appears to be a little untidy, with the first three buttons hanging loose. This reveals a dark purple bruise running like a line across his neck. She curiously yet fearfully looks at the man, swearing he too seems familiar from family photo albums. The man is no other than Louis Fisher. Suddenly, he disappears into thin air. Annabelle looks at the now-sitting Henry to empty her mind and stop dwelling on whether or not the ghost of Louis is present. She then turns to Eden, who is so beautiful and has a gracious smile that can brighten an entire room. Annabelle happily admires this for a while.

A waiter noticeably older than the previous one approaches the table and begins pouring champagne into flutes. With the departure of the waiter, Martin stands.

"I would like to congratulate Henry and Eden for the beginning of their own family, and I would also like to say Louis would be so happy and proud of what you've achieved, Henry. I'm sure Louis is here with us in spirit tonight."

Judging by the lack of reaction, it seems no one knows of Louis' presence. Annabelle finds it funny in an irony kind of way for her great-great-grandfather to say Louis is here in the figural sense. Annabelle watches her distant family toast and drinking their champagne. She takes a small sip of her golden bubbly drink. The younger waiter arrives at the table carrying three dishes. He briefly leaves and then returns about three more times with dishes. With hot steamy food in front of each person they all begin to eat.

Annabelle looks up from her food to find Samuel, sitting directly opposite to her, raising his eyebrow, which she reads it as him checking her out. She quickly bows her head to avoid awkwardness.

"I have no doubt you two are going to be great parents," Stella says.

"Thank you, Mother."

"The baby makes me think of a memory when Henry was about a year old. It was his first time on a ship, which was in the Belfast Harbour. He ran up and down along the deck with a big happy smile on his face. As I recall, Louis was there that day," Meredith says.

"He sure was. I believe the sea trials for the ocean liner were due to start later that day," Edward says.

Silence follows with people either chewing or cutting at their food. Having dinner with family has Annabelle remembering dinner with the Remals three nights ago, though it feels like years ago now. A cold shiver, deep to the bone, seemingly from nowhere, runs through Annabelle. This is when she notices the silhouette of a hand flat on the table beside her own. She shoots a jumpy look up and sees Louis standing in the small wedge beside her. Small chattering begins from the table, but Annabelle fixates on Louis and therefore doesn't listen to the conversation.

Louis doesn't appear to be in any pain; nor does he have growing anger that will eventually lash and intend to harm someone. He smiles at her while she nervously smiles back at him. It's almost like he's specifically here to tell her something, but what? Without saying a single word, he disappears again. Annabelle turns her head so it aligns with the rest of her body and continues to eat. Chewing on a mouthful, she looks around and sees everyone else finishing up on their meals. The clanging of cutlery against the porcelain plates quietens.

"That certainly hit the spot," George says.

"Yes, indeed, splendid," Fredrick says.

"So is everyone packed and ready for the voyage tomorrow?" Samuel asks.

Everyone, out of synch, mutters, "Yes."

"I look forward to sailing upon *Marida*," Evelyn says.

The mention of *Marida* has Annabelle thinking of the newspaper article regarding the night of Henry and Eden's eightieth wedding anniversary.

"Dear, we better get going. Tomorrow's a big day, particularly for you," Stella says.

Martin stands and then aids his wife up. Evelyn also stands.

"Very well. I'll see all of you tomorrow. Thank you for your company. Goodnight," Martin says.

Stella and Evelyn say goodbye before leaving the table with Martin. Edward and then Meredith stand.

"We better get going ourselves. Thank you for the company at dinner, and I shall see you tomorrow," Edward says before he and Meredith leave.

"Seems like it's our turn to leave," Henry says.

"If you like I could escort Annabelle to the car," Samuel says.

"Certainly, why not?" Henry says.

Annabelle feels a little unsure because of the awkward look from Samuel earlier. Henry, Samuel, Eden and Annabelle all stand and say bye to Fredrick and George, the last remaining people at the table. The two Delighkan brothers escort the ladies towards the exit.

"I hope you weren't checking me out, like finding me attracting."

"Well, you are quite beaut—"

"We're related," Annabelle quickly interrupts.

"How come we've never met? How are we related?"

"It would make less sense if I told you."

Samuel scrunches his face with confusion.

"Did you see Louis Fisher? At one point he was standing beside me, you still didn't see him?"

"No, are you OK?"

"I do feel a little weird, seeing these unexplainable things that have been happening all day. I'm sorry to burden you with my troubles."

"It's OK. Saying your troubles aloud may help you solve them. Even though I don't know a thing about your weird occurrences, the simplest explanation coming to my mind is it's a dream."

They exit the restaurant and join Henry and Eden out on the street. There's a slight chill as Annabelle adjusts to the different temperature. Henry, Eden, and Annabelle say bye to Samuel as they hop into Henry's automobile. The interior is dark and cosy. Putting along Henry drives a semicircle around the town garden before turning down Grand Ocean Road.

The dim headlights provide limited visibility along the pitch-black road. The quarter-phase moon hangs above the calm ocean. Annabelle looks towards the shoreline and notices the tugboat missing. She intensely keeps her eyes on the travelling shore, confirming the little maroon tugboat is no longer there. She assumes the waves have carried it out to sea.

At the home stretch, the automobile travels up the smooth, lengthy driveway. Pulling up, everyone hops out and enters the house. Mollie greets in the doorway. The home is bright and welcoming.

"Thank you very much for dinner tonight," Annabelle says.

"You're welcome," Henry says.

"Seeing that it's a beautiful clear night, I'm going out on the balcony. I know Henry will join me. Would you like to, Annabelle?"

"No, thanks. I'm beat, so I might go to bed."

"Very well. After stargazing, I would love to accompany you for a cup of tea, Mollie."

"Certainly, ma'am. I'll boil the kettle." Mollie walks off.

Henry and Eden say goodnight to Annabelle and then head up the stairs. She watches them reach the top of the staircase. Taking about three steps up the stairs, she suddenly feels something pulling at her skin on the left side of her forehead, kind of like the sensation of ripping off a bandage. Just adding to the list of weirdness, she brushes it off and continues up the stairs.

Seeing the glass doors open, Annabelle inconspicuously peers out. Henry and Eden stand close as they lean against the chunky railing. They look up at the sky while their inner hands rest upon each other on top of the railing. Overseeing this brings peace to Annabelle. Beginning to feel the strain of her tiring body, she walks along the hallway and enters the same guest room from earlier.

The bright hallway light streams into the room. The turned-down bed is ready for sleep. She shuts the door and throws her body onto the bed in the now pitch-black room. Within minutes, she starts to drift off to sleep.

CHAPTER 7

The night sky cloaks the nearby island of Suntree Bay, and they anchor down the *Marida* in the marina. The choppy sea creates a bumpy ride on the vessel. Five-year-old Annabelle runs happily along the deck with her short tight curls flopping and her yellow flowery party dress flouncing. This part of the ship is quiet and empty. Reaching the end of the boat deck, she meets up with one-hundred-year-old Henry and Eden. They look so presentable in a tuxedo and a flowing white sequence dress. Eden creakily bends down and hands her journal to Annabelle.

"Hold on to this for me, please. You can return it later when you go to our place."

Annabelle smiles as she hugs the journal.

"Don't wander too far. We'll go back to the party together soon," Henry says.

"OK, Grandpa Henry."

Not wandering far, she reaches a nearby deck chair and climbs up with the journal still in her grip. Her great-grandparents are at a bit of a distance, but she's within earshot of them. Henry and Eden look out to the glowing Suntree Bay.

"Would you believe it was eighty years ago on this very deck that I proposed to you?"

"I couldn't be any happier for all the time we have spent together since then."

They turn to each other, give a quick, passionate kiss and then wrap their arms around each other. The winds begin to pick up with a growing force. The *Marida* is increasingly knocking about.

Annabelle watches her mother, Heather—a firm build with a tight black dress and her long brunet hair in a bun—approach Henry and Eden. They break apart from their hug and face Heather.

"My heart was broken; now it's your turn." Heather stabs Henry in the chest.

After seconds of holding it there, she retracts the knife and runs off. Henry holds onto his bleeding chest as he drops to the deck floor. Eden weightlessly drops down and kneels beside Henry. They stare at each other in what seems like forever. Annabelle sits on the deck chair in silence, trying to understand the scene taking place. By having a front-row seat, Annabelle can just see Henry's eyes close, as if he's drifting off to sleep.

"Henry!" Eden screams with deep pain.

Eden grabs Henry's hand as she sobs over him. Annabelle remains objective as she curiously continues to watch on. The big part she's having trouble understanding is why her mother would do this. Heather is a kind and nurturing type of mum who wouldn't seem like the one to harm anyone. She slides down from the deck chair and dawdles in the direction of her mother. Walking along a few paces, she sees no one. She decides to turn around and head back. Suddenly, a massive knock from the rough sea throws the *Marida* halfway to an upward angle.

At a short distance, Annabelle watches her great-grandfather sliding overboard. The *Marida* levels out. Eden struggles to her feet, her wrinkle face red from tears. She steps to the deck's ledge and peers down.

"Grandma?" Annabelle questions Eden's actions.

Eden looks up at Annabelle. She smiles under her sorrows and then leaps overboard.

"Eden!"

Like waking from a nightmare, Annabelle jolts up in a freak panic. She hyperventilates when discovering she's in a hospital bed. Wanda springs up from a nearby chair and tries to calm her sister.

"I need to talk to Eden. I saw it," Annabelle says, not calming down at all.

"Annabelle, calm down."

"Why am I in hospital?"

"You've been in a coma for about two days. An elderly lady found you in the lounge."

Learning this information, Annabelle calmly slows her breathing as she pensively thinks. Everything makes logic sense now. She just needs something to help her verify this logic sense.

"Where's my handbag?"

"In the drawer beside you." Wanda points to the tiny two drawer bedside table.

Annabelle twists her upper body and opens the top drawer. She pulls out her handbag, repositions herself, and immediately unbuttons it. Firstly, the bag itself proves something. Initially, Annabelle lost her bag at sea during the tugboat incident. She pulls out her phone and looks at its side. With an analysing squint, she discovers a microscopic drop of blood. She feels the left side of her forehead and gently rubs the soft gauze.

"I better get the doctor now." Wanda walks out of the room.

Annabelle looks around her small private hospital room and spots a dress draping over a plastic chair with vinyl padding. She slowly pulls out the stingy IV needle, fumbles off the bed, and stumbles over to the chair. Throwing off the hospital gown and slipping on her strap polka-dot dress, tucks her feet in black slip on shoes she finds under the chair and then grabs her phone and bag from the bed. Annabelle casually walks out of the room in order to avoid attention.

Wanda enters the room accompanied by a slightly plump middle-aged man. His identification tag with his mugshot-looking photo and "Dr. N. Melave" underneath is hanging from his chest pocket of his lab coat. Not seeing Annabelle on the bed, Wanda panics as she rushes to the nearby corner and checks out the hidden toilet cubicle.

"Annabelle's not here," Wanda says after popping out from the cubicle.

"I'll alert security."

"Knowing how stubborn and determine she is, I guarantee she wouldn't be in the hospital. My best guess is she's gone to the Delighkan House. Apparently, she saw it and needs to tell Eden, whatever that means."

"Are you referring to your great-grandmother who went missing twenty years ago?"

Wanda nods.

"Is this what she said when she first woke up?"

Wanda nods again.

"It sounds like a suppressed memory possibly woke her from the coma. If she's unwilling to come back here, I strongly recommend for you to stay with her and make sure she's OK."

"OK, thank you very much. Bye."

Wanda leaves, walking hurriedly along the quiet corridor. Pressing the down button, she waits anxiously for the elevator doors to open. The elevator ride is uneventful. It arrives around the corner from the lobby. The waiting area is ordinary with the abundance of chairs, piles of magazines resting on a couple of small tables and medical posters of either anatomy diagrams or instructions for emergency situations. Walking past the receptionist hiding behind a glass window and with her head down, Wanda exits the hospital.

She hops into her Corolla on the side of the street. Quickly gearing up, she takes off. Being only a little after seven o'clock in the morning, light traffic begins to flow along the growing streets. She drives around the town garden and makes her way down Grand Ocean Road. During her travels, the only thing she has on her mind is Annabelle. Is she OK? If she is indeed at the Delighkan House, how did she get there? These troubling questions worry Wanda.

Making her way up the smooth lengthy driveway, she's just in time to see Annabelle enter the house. Wanda rushes out of the car and darts to the front door. Annabelle stands in the middle of the foyer looking up towards the top of the staircase. Then, her head begins to gradually tilt downward, appearing as if she's watching someone walk down the stairs. The head movement suggests that

Eden could be travelling along the staircase, but Wanda doesn't see anything. The other suggestion could be Annabelle is imagining things as a result of being in the coma. Even with her sceptical doubts, Wanda is hopeful that Eden is present.

Suddenly Annabelle drops to the floor like dead weight. Wanda dashes to her and kneels beside her. Annabelle doesn't look well at all. She's profusely sweating, her face bright red from exhaustion, and her deep sinking chest is breathless. Annabelle stares at the empty space at the base of the staircase. She smiles as her breathing begins to catch up. Wanda assumes Eden is standing there, but she still doesn't see anything.

"Would you like to go back to the hospital?"

Annabelle drops her smile and shakes her head.

"I'll at least take you to your place. That way, you can get all dressed up and ready for tonight."

"Is it the third of September today?"

"It sure is. You woke up just in time."

Annabelle slowly begins to wobble to her feet. Wanda grabs hold of her and steadily aids her. With Wanda continuing to aid Annabelle, they slowly make their way to the open front door.

"By the way, how did you get here?" Wanda asks, stopping in the doorway.

"I ran."

Annabelle slouches on her grey two-seat sofa. The eighty-centimetre LCD television directly in front of the sofa blares. Wanda sits up straight as she fully views the screen, whereas Annabelle only pays half of the attention. The need to visit Eden busily dominates her thoughts. The image now on the television screen is of a young woman reporter with the gum tree from the town garden in the background.

"Everything is getting ready and set up for tonight's festivities to celebrate the centenary anniversary of Suntree Bay. On this very evening one hundred years ago, Henry and Eden Delighkan shared the grand opening and their wedding with their fellow guests. On this night only twenty years ago during the Delighkan's eightieth wedding anniversary celebration aboard the S. S. *Marida*, they mysteriously disappeared. People have claimed to have seen the ghost of Eden wandering throughout the abandoned Delighkan House, but due to a lack of proof, this claim is nothing more than the town's local legend. What did happen to the Delighkans on that fateful night? No one knows. In other news, the S. S. *Marida* is ready for its first voyage in twenty years, departing at noon tomorrow. It is said the vessel was initially taken out of service due to the Delighkans' disappearance. With the milestone anniversary afoot and two whole decades having passed, the Delighkan Family has decided to put the *Marida* back in service. This is Lauren Ashburn, reporting live from the town garden. Back to you."

A slightly older woman in a newsroom says, "We'll report back later with Lauren Ashburn. See you after the break." Then the television cuts to advertisements. Wanda mutters along to a jingling food advertisement. Annabelle looks over to a three shelf bookcase. There's a dome clock sitting on top. The time is 3:45.

"It's about an hour away this thing technically starts, isn't it?"

Wanda nods after looking at the same clock.

"I just had a mind blank. I'm supposed to be delivering a speech."

"The council exempted you from it because of your coma."

"I'm OK to do it. I've just been preoccupied with the Delighkan House and Eden's journal and haven't given the speech much thought."

Wanda's phone rings. She pulls it out from her tight little handbag and answers it. Annabelle switches the television off.

"I'm still at Annabelle's."

Annabelle begins to fidget with her growing restless fingers while listening to half of the conversation.

"I'll be there soon. Bye." Wanda hangs up the phone and shoves it back in her handbag.

"What's going on?"

"That was Steve. He's needed at the pier to do last minute things to the *Marida*, so I need to go home and take care of Mitch. I suppose with only an hour left I better go and get ready too," Wanda stands and heads towards the nearby front door.

"Just curious, has my car been here the whole time?"

"No, it was at the Delighkan House, Steve drove it back here. Speaking of driving, can you please, please stay here and I'll come back here later to get you and take you to the town garden."

"Fine, I will. Maybe I should think about my speech."

"You do that." Wanda walks out through the screen door.

Annabelle sits silently, Eden instantly racing into her mind. Then, she shoots a look over at the bookcase with the clock on top. She springs up, grabs a small hardcover book from the top shelf and sits back on the sofa. The title is *Urban Folklore* and even though it's a fictional fairy-tale type book, she recalls at the end, one tale that tells about laws ghosts abide by. Flipping through three-quarters of the way, she finds the page. She begins to read, mouthing the words while doing so.

"Of course, Eden must be attached to her journal, which she told me to return when I went back to her place. This is why she haunts the house and not where she died."

Recounting, she remembers the reflection in the window. There's definitely a ghost present in the hotel's lounge.

"Henry's got to be in the lounge, but what would he be attached to?"

Continuing to read on until she reaches the end of the page, her excitement heightens.

"Ghost possession. That'll be interesting." She slams the book shut.

Placing the book beside her, she notices her body odour.

"I better pretty myself up for the big celebration."

Looking over at the clock, the time reads a little before 4:00 p.m. She springs to her feet again and enters the minuscule bathroom. The lukewarm running water is refreshing. Slipping out of the shower, she hurriedly dries herself and wraps the towel around her skinny torso and enters the neighbouring bedroom. She drops the towel and throws on a bright, flouncy dress she pulls out from her wardrobe. A couple items of silver jewellery and faintly painting her face, and she's ready to go.

Annabelle exits the bedroom, grabs her handbag, and rushes out the front door. She hops into her CR-V and then backs out of the driveway. Turning down that street and then turning down another, she makes her way through the urban maze. Passing the smooth, lengthy driveway leading to the Delighkan House, she now turns onto Grand Ocean Road. The low-afternoon sun bounces off the seemingly always calm ocean. Annabelle ends her trip by parking directly in front of the hotel.

CHAPTER 8

Annabelle revolves into the hotel lobby. At least a dozen or so people occupy this space, loudly engaging in conversations. It's typically busy in the hotel this time every year, seeing that the town does something to commemorate the anniversary, which is the reason why the ferry would be delivering visitors to the island round about now. This is the busiest yet, probably due to the big one.

A young man, wearing a tuxedo and his black hair slicked back, stands behind the concierge desk. This is Pete. His duties seem to be overwhelming him as he deals with three people in front of him and answering the phone. Annabelle usually works this shift, but for obvious reasons, she's not working today. Appearing from nowhere, Robert Gendrick tends to the three people in front of the desk. Pete places the phone back on the hook. Annabelle leans against the concierge desk. Pete smiles upon seeing her. They talk loud to compete with the increasing volume.

"Hello, nice to see you up and about. How are you?"

"I'm fine. I feel like I just woke up from a really long nap. Say, you look smart in that tuxedo."

"Thanks. You look pretty smart yourself."

"Thank you. Hey, do you need any help? You look a little swamped."

"No, it's OK. You're probably busy preparing what to say tonight."

"Obviously, my speech is no secret."

"Of course. Which other Delighkan would be best to do it?"

"Well, I'd better get going. I'll surely see you later."

Pete quickly waves and then answers the ringing phone. Annabelle walks away.

She enters the pleasantly quiet lounge. No one else is in here.

"Henry, are you here?"

There's no response. She dawdles over to the fireplace. Her eyes observe Star's wand sitting perfectly in the centre of the mantelpiece. Her sight wanders up at the painting of the *Marida* beside Suntree Bay. Maintaining her wandering eyesight, she draws attention to the nearby glary window. Moving in front of the window, she rubs her bandage. Standing in the same spot she recalls that moment— blacking out, the phone on the floor, and the reflection of the figure. Suddenly, the figure's reflection appears again in the window. She nervously bolts around to find her mother, Heather. Without giving her a second glance, Annabelle returns her attention to the window.

"Hey, sweetie, you look like you're feeling better."

The transparent reflection is oddly confusing. It appears to be the same figure from earlier, and yet, it's her mother who stands behind her, casting the reflection. Annabelle finally turns around and looks at Heather unsurely.

"Are you all right?" Heather's smile drops as she expresses concern.

"When did you get back from your holiday?"

"Two days ago. It was actually the same morning you went into your coma."

"Where did you and Dad go?"

"You should know. It has been an annual trip since you and Wanda were kids."

"Just enlighten me, where, exactly?"

"We stayed in the old family mansion in Cobh, Ireland."

"So I assume it was around this time of year in 1993 you went to Cobh," Annabelle says while thinking of the moment Heather stabs Henry and realising the act was indeed of spiritual possession.

"Yes, I remember the ferry arriving at port only just in time for the anniversary party."

"Your maiden name being Fisher is the last piece of the puzzle in order for this to make sense. I think I know what happened. Now I really need to talk to Grandma Eden," Annabelle excitedly hypes.

"Are you sure you're OK? You know it's not possible to talk to Grandma Eden, right?"

"I need you to just trust me." Annabelle grabs her mother's hand.

They walk out of the lounge and continue their way through the busy lobby. No time for distractions or detours as they quickly revolve out of the hotel individually.

They hop into the CR-V and drive off. The car turns down Grand Ocean Road. Moderate traffic flows along this road as the dimming afternoon sun hangs low. The two women momentarily sit in silence.

"So I'm guessing that his suicide is the reason why he wouldn't be at rest and being dead since 1913 might have made his spirit angry, which would explain why he hitched a ride from Cobh and killed Henry. If this is the case, I somewhat feel sorry for Louis," Annabelle rambles.

Loud static comes over the radio as though there's electrical interference. The air in the car suddenly turns cold almost as if the air conditioning is operating. Annabelle feels the car beginning to accelerate out of her control. She turns to her mother, who is looking blankly out of the windshield. The possession is happening again.

"Louis, can you hear me?"

The CR-V picks up more speed. In a frantic panic, she watches the speedometer's needle spiking.

"Sorry, Mum," Annabelle says with slight hesitance.

She forcefully punches Heather in the nose, knocking her out immediately. Annabelle feels herself in control of the car just in time to yank the wheel and steer up the smooth lengthy driveway. Not braking hard enough in order to slow from the incredible speed, the CR-V crashes into the front doorway of the Delighkan House.

The collision causes the front door's surrounding wall to shatter, and the CR-V comes to an abrupt halt about a foot away from the base of the staircase. The impact sends debris flying. Annabelle busts her lower lip against the steering wheel. Feeling a little faint, she looks over at her mother, who remains unconscious. Heather has the tiniest blob of blood leaking out of one nostril, most likely from the punch. There are no other physical signs of injury as far as Annabelle can tell.

"Mum, can you hear me?"

No response. Annabelle steadily opens the car door and fumbles out of the vehicle. She stumbles to the side of the hood and leans against it. Sunlight beams into the foyer kind of like a spotlight. The car seems to be the only one who didn't sustain any injuries. Overcoming slight disorientation, she looks about midway up the stairs.

There's a woman who appears to be in her fifties. She's wearing a long dress, dating to the time Annabelle identifies as the period of Eden's youth. Her thick black hair is in a bun, and her pale white skin is nearly transparent. Annabelle looks on in awe as she now recognises the woman. It's Annie Fisher. Annabelle observes Annie's expression, interpreting it as confusion and guilt. Eden appears beside Annie. She looks so youthful and somehow lively as she smiles down at Annabelle.

"Eden, I'm sorry. I can't explain my intentions."

Eden looks at Annie while maintaining her smile.

"I can explain."

Both ghosts look down at Annabelle who now stands independently.

"When you died, you were at peace, on the pretence you were going to find Louis. Unfortunately, you didn't. You grew angry and repeatedly possessed my mother in order to escape the old family mansion. I know the love you have for Louis due to family stories that have been passed down the generations. You would never want to harm anyone because you have too much of a caring soul for that."

"It's OK, Annie, and I forgive you. I will be with Henry, as you will soon be with Louis."

Annabelle watches on, slightly smiling with contentment. The two ladies hug and suddenly vanish into thin air. Annabelle's face drops. She narrowly squeezes by the hood of the car and hurries about halfway up the staircase.

"Annie, Eden, where are you?" Annabelle looks around.

Eden's journal is laying on the one step above. Annabelle slowly bends down and picks it up. An aching groan breaks the silence.

"Hang on, Mum. I'm coming," Annabelle hurries back down the stairs.

She slips into the driver's seat just in time to see Heather gaining consciousness. Heather's head drops a little as she turns it to the side. This motion is like turning on a tap, as it causes a sudden gushing nosebleed. Her immediate reaction is tilting her head slightly upward. Annabelle quickly throws Eden's journal on the dashboard and presses a button on the car door as she hops out. Pulling open the glass window of the boot, she grabs a full roll of toilet paper that casually happens to be there. She slams the boot shut, returns to the driver's seat and instantly shoves the roll of paper under her mother's nose. Heather raises an odd eyebrow towards Annabelle.

"You never know when you've got to go."

Heather lightly chuckles. Annabelle gently pulls the roll of paper away and notices the nosebleed barely being a drip.

"How's it looking, Doc?"

"You've lost a fair bit of blood. The bleeding looks like it has stopped."

"Are you going to tell me what just happened?"

Annabelle places the soaked roll on the middle console.

"Well, it might be hard to believe."

"I'm pretty open-minded. Tell me."

"Maybe later, once I have all the facts straight."

"OK, can you at least tell me that we're going to the town garden?"

"That I can do." Annabelle pulls the car door shut.

She starts the engine and gracefully backs out of the house with no troubles. Idling in front of the house she distastefully looks at the gaping car-size hole and the debris covering the floor. It's quite upsetting to see the historic house sitting in its current state.

"My house," Annabelle sadly says.

"Your house?" Heather questions.

"It's rightfully mine, and I've really grown fond of it, enough to live here."

"I love what you've done with the place."

By now, the last remnants of sunlight fade from against the Delighkan House, leaving the building in the shadowing darkness. Annabelle does a U-turn and drives down the smooth, lengthy driveway. She switches the headlights on as dusk sets in. The CR-V makes its way along Grand Ocean Road.

"Just curious, was Grandma Annie still alive when you were born?" Annabelle asks.

"I think I was about three years old. I could've sworn I was older, though. I remember visiting family in the old mansion when I was about eight, and I saw Grandma Annie and actually spoke to her too. When I told Dad about this, he just referred to her as an imaginary friend."

"That makes sense."

"OK, whatever you say."

"Annie connected with you after becoming a ghost, which is probably the reason why she chose to possess you."

"What?"

Annabelle thinks of the idea of a ghost somewhat befriending a family member. Similarly, this seems to be the case towards Eden; Annabelle would like to think so. With the deepening thoughts occupying her mind, she decides to turn on the radio. Funnily this makes her a more attentive driver, as music generally disables her thinking, which is more distracting than noise.

Reaching the end of Grand Ocean Road she turns right onto the connecting street and then parks directly in front of the hotel. She turns the car off and looks over at Heather.

"Wait a minute." Annabelle pulls out a travel-size packet of baby wipes from the glove box. "You've got a little blood stuck to your nose."

"You're equipped and ready for anything," Heather says while taking a cloth from the packet and wiping her nose.

"Well, I often have Mitch with me."

Heather opens the door.

"Mum, are you feeling OK?"

"I'm fine."

"OK, I'll catch up with you later."

Heather hops out of the car and shuts the door. Soon after, Annabelle follows suit. The town garden is stunning. Multi-coloured lanterns suspending from nearly invisible wiring connecting to skinny metal poles create a semicircle barrier around the grassy area. A slightly elevating platform stage is in the corner of the garden, about twenty feet or so in front of the hotel. A long extending buffet table with a wide variety of scrumptious food sits in the opposite corner from the stage. Glittering fairy lights makes the gum tree glow. An abundant crowd of people flood the entire area. All of this enhances the already naturally beautiful garden.

Wanda is currently in the centre of the stage. The band consisting of drums, guitars, and a keyboard play behind her. She sings along to the beat. The music is upbeat and groovy, provoking dancing and cheering. The atmosphere feels great and enjoyable. Annabelle approaches the stage and slowly steps up from the side as the song concludes. The two sisters stand side by side as the crowd cheers.

"Where have you been and why do you have a busted up lip?" Wanda asks while maintaining her smiling attention to her fellow people.

"Is now the appropriate time for getting angry with me?"

The crowd now quietens. Annabelle pulls the wireless microphone off the stand.

"Hello, Suntree Bay. We're the Delighkan sisters, and we are proud to celebrate the grand centenary anniversary with you tonight. It's hard to believe exactly one hundred years ago, in this very spot, our great-grandparents, Henry and Eden Delighkan, founders of Suntree Bay, celebrated the grand opening of the island and also honoured their love, with their wedding. I take it everyone knows of the local legend. Henry and Eden mysteriously disappeared in 1993, exactly twenty years ago. At the time, they were aboard the S. S. *Marida*, celebrating their eightieth wedding anniversary. I've been recently doing a little bit of research, and I discovered something huge. There is more to the legend no one knows about. There was a lost soul wandering from decades ago. This soul was angry and confused, and so it ended up killing Henry. The rough, choppy sea that night knocked Henry's dead body overboard. Eden, dearly loving Henry, couldn't live without him, so she jumped overboard. But let's not dwell on their grim end. Let's celebrate the great legacy they left behind. Lastly, the *Marida* will be sailing for the first time in twenty years. In a matter of speaking, if it weren't for that ship, Suntree Bay wouldn't be here today."

A couple of firing rockets explode in the sky above the *Marida* down at the marina, about two kilometres away. The aftermath of the rocket brightly showers down, enhancing the already glowing grand vessel.

"So, in the comfort of great music, food, and people, enjoy the rest of the evening."

The crowd loudly applauds. Wanda and Annabelle step off the stage. Their parents, Bill and Heather, meet them nearby.

"Hello, Annabelle. Glad to see you up and about." Bill hugs his daughter.

"Nice to see you back home from your holiday."

"I'm happy to see you doing OK. It's quite shocking to come home from a holiday to find your daughter in a coma," Heather says.

"Sorry about that."

"How did you find out about Henry and Eden?" Wanda asks.

"I found out from the Delighkan House and Eden's journal."

"There's something else, isn't there?"

"Nope, that's the whole story. I'm feeling peckish. Excuse me."

The band on stage begins playing again, this time with a young man on vocals. Annabelle walks away, avoiding explaining the whole Annie and possession ordeal, at least for now. She approaches the buffet table. About a dozen peckish people pick from the table.

Carefully surveying the scrumptious food, she considers what to have. She picks up a mini quiche and takes a bite. This sends her stomach into a churning frenzy as she realises she has not really eaten for days. Steve and Mitch come up to Annabelle. Mitch is wearing a black vest suit with a bow tie, which immediately draws her attention.

"Hi there, Annabelle," Steve says.

"Hello, Aunt Anna."

"Hello guys, you look so handsome in your little suit."

"Thanks, I did dress myself," Steve jokes.

Annabelle raises her eyebrow at Steve who wears something similar to Mitch but doesn't pull it off as handsomely as the little boy.

"Mitch wanted to hang with you for a bit. Is that OK?"

"Sure."

"You behave for Aunt Anna." Steve taps Mitch on the shoulder. "Catch up with you two later."

"Are you hungry? Here try one of these. They're nice." Annabelle picks up a mini quiche and hands it to Mitch.

Mitch munches on it, seemingly enjoying it. Annabelle looks out at the *Marida*. This reminds her she's yet to find Henry. Not being the ghost in the lounge, he has to be on the *Marida*. She kneels down to be eye level with Mitch.

"Hey mate, do you want to go somewhere cool?

He happily nods.

"Seeing that you so bravely entered the haunted Delighkan House, you can handle encountering a ghost on a ship, right?"

He nods again, not with as much enthusiasm but still happy.

"Let's go." Annabelle rises and grabs Mitch's arm.

They step off the perimeter of the town garden and head right on the street.

"Where are you guys off to?"

Annabelle and Mitch turn around to find Wanda.

"We're going somewhere cool," Mitch says.

"Yeah, I thought it'll be cool to take Mitch aboard the *Marida*. I was thinking about heading up onto the boat deck."

"Wow, that does sound cool. Maybe after a bite to eat, I could meet you up there. I wouldn't mind checking out the *Marida* myself."

"Sounds great. I'll see you up there."

Annabelle and Mitch continue their travels. Following along the street, they step over the railway crossing that seamlessly runs through. After about a kilometre or so, they reach the marina. The *Marida* has company with the ferry nearby and a few small private yachts. The thirty-foot-wide wooden dock runs along the shoreline. The front-and-centre *Marida* parallel to the dock is the first vessel to encounter. Annabelle spots two sailors on the dock not far from the gangplank leading to the *Marida*'s open entrance door.

"I'm sorry, would it be possible to board the *Marida*, or am I pushing the boundary?"

"Not at all, Miss Delighkan. Go ahead."

"Thanks."

Annabelle and Mitch walk along the gangplank. Upon entering the ship, they step into a wide corridor. The rowing light fixtures along the wall brighten the area and reveal a cushioning carpet runner and a golden frame two-seat lounge sitting against the wall nearby. About six feet to the right is the lift lobby. A few paces to the left, there's a massive archway. They continue their travels under the archway and find the D-deck stairwell.

It's in a huge open area that's bright from the little crystal chandeliers populating the ceiling. The white glow from the chandeliers makes the hard white floor gloss and the nearby oak walls to shine. Passing thin oak pillars, they begin making their way up the staircase.

Reaching C-deck, they loop around and continue their climb to the next level. Maintaining their pace they make it to B-deck. After climbing three stairwells, they finally reach A-deck. Standing at the very top of the stairwell the open area looks quite similar in design to D-deck. She briefly stops and admires the craftsmanship of the stairwell, noticing now that it's nearly identical to the staircase in the hotel's lobby. On the right and slightly around the corner, there's a wooden panel glass door. They open it and walk through.

Annabelle and Mitch are now on the boat deck. She looks around fully attentive, expecting Henry to be here. The ocean is calm as it gently breaks against the *Marida*'s hull. The air is cool with the slightest breeze.

"Here, kid. Check out the awesome view of Suntree Bay from here." Annabelle guides Mitch over to the ledge of the boat deck, where the row of lifeboats begin.

The music is audible from afar as the band starts a new song. He looks out at the lively town that stands about two kilometres away. Annabelle stands beside Mitch. It's quite peaceful looking at the island from here. She contently looks down at Mitch, and out the corner of her eye, suddenly spots a silhouetted hand resting on Mitch's shoulder. Freaking, she frantically scans the deck. No one else is here. She turns back to the Welcoming Suntree Bay and begins to calm a little, bracing herself as she waits for Henry.

CHAPTER 9

The cool breezy air noticeably turns chilly and stiff. Annabelle steps away from the edge and slowly turns around. Henry, appearing clearly and youthful, gives a grieving look. Annabelle stares deep into his graceful eyes. Not being able to pull her attention away, she fixates on Henry. He slowly moves to the edge of the deck and stands in the exact spot from 1993. Flashes of Henry and Eden's fate haunt Annabelle's mind. The ending of the deck doesn't stop Henry continuing on. He then stands in mid-air. Annabelle looks over the ledge in astonishment as Henry levitates at least forty feet above the water while the edge of the dock is about ten feet away from the *Marida*'s hull. Henry suddenly vanishes from sight. In the hopes that Henry is back on deck, she swiftly looks around behind her. There's no Henry, though she does see Wanda coming on deck via the glass door. Not thinking logically and only thinking of finding Henry, Annabelle leaps overboard.

"Annabelle!" Wanda screams.

The cold water is piercing. The eternal darkness looms as she slowly sinks in the heavy and suffocating sea. With determination she forcefully breaches the stiff surface. Kicking and splashing, she swims poorly towards a nearby ladder at the end of the dock. Climbing up onto the dock she immediately spots Henry on the shoreline as he begins to head towards Suntree Bay. Annabelle hurriedly walks along the dock and then heads up the street. Maintaining her pace up the street she suddenly screams from excruciating jolts, as though something is frying her entire body with electricity. This throws her flat on her back against the tar surface. Feeling weak to the bone, she manages to wobble onto her feet. Looking down, it seems the only culprit for the electrifying surprise is the railway track.

"What the …?" Annabelle asks while curiously squinting down at the tracks.

Taking a couple of paces back, she leaps over the track and continues on her way.

The town garden continues its lively upbeat celebration. Annabelle wanders in among the spacious crowd. People must be really into the festivities because everyone seems to be oblivious to Annabelle's presence. She can feel something like an essence, which lures her in a particular direction. Making it out of the crowd, she discovers Henry sitting on the park bench under the gum tree. He's accompanied by who appears to be Louis Fisher. As Annabelle recalls he looks the same as his cameo appearance in her coma.

"Hello, Annabelle. It's nice for you to join us. I've been waiting for you," Louis says.

"Have you been here the whole time?" Annabelle curiously asks.

"I've been around, though I do come to this very spot every year and lure Henry to accompany me."

"It's quite a delight to observe my grand town every year for its anniversary," Henry says.

She listens to the two gentlemen, forgetting the fact she's talking to ghosts.

"You managed to get Henry away from the place where he died. How did you do that?"

"Being an earthbound spirit for close to one hundred years, I've picked up a few things."

"That explains why I saw you while I was in a coma."

Louis stands while Henry remains on the bench.

"Sorry if I spooked you, I saw your unconscious state as an opportunity to make contact. Now, take my hand. I need to show you something." Louis holds out his right hand.

Without hesitation, she willingly grabs his hand. Everything fades to a pure white glow.

Annabelle is standing presumably near the B-deck stairwell on the *Marida*. Louis appears from nowhere as he stands beside her.

"Jeez, no more spooky surprises," Annabelle says, a little jumpy.

"Sorry, I'll try to keep it at least to the bare minimum."

A handsome man wearing formal attire escorts a beautiful lady in a long gleaming gown. The couple abruptly stop in their travels. This is when Annabelle recognises them as Louis and Annie Fisher. She shoots a look of confusion towards Louis the ghost.

"Why are there two of you?"

"One such thing I've picked up is the ability to visit my past memories."

"So where and when are we?"

"We're aboard the SS *Neris* on the ninth of March, 1912."

"The *Neris*—that sounds familiar."

"It's the *Marida*'s sister ship."

Annabelle falls quiet, dreadfully realising this is the ship that eventually leads to Louis' suicide. She shoots her attention back to the lively couple overhearing Annie's comment.

"I never grow tired at gazing upon this magnificent staircase. I find it to be one of the highlights of the entire ship."

"Yes, and I do believe Henry largely had an input in the design of this area," the past Louis says.

After a moment of admiring the staircase, the couple continues on their way. Annabelle smiles as she watches the couple head off, not thinking of their future. Instead, she thinks of their present.

"Seeing that we're in the year 1912, can we check out another ship?" Annabelle bubbly asks.

"I'm sorry, but I was never aboard that vessel, so I, therefore, don't have any memories to visit."

"That's a bummer."

Louis gently grabs hold of Annabelle's hand. In an instant, they're somewhere else, on the forward section of the bow, to be exact. Thick heavy fog cloaks the blinding air. Only about two square feet of the deck is visible. The open sea is presumably out there as it sloshes against the *Neris*'s hull.

"It's quite peaceful to be wandering about the ship this time of night, once everyone retires to their cabins."

"That's great. Well, I think I've almost got the hang of this teleporting," Annabelle says while hanging onto the nearby railing.

She throws half her body as she feels like she's about to vomit. It's a false alarm. Fixing herself to an upright position, she spots the past Louis and Annie close by. Annabelle steps closer to Annie. She doesn't at all react to Annabelle's presence.

"I suppose she can't see me."

"Think of this as a recollection and not an event happening now."

Louis the ghost and Annabelle observe the couple like watching a play at the theatre.

"I've never seen fog this thick out at sea before," Annie says.

"I must agree, and I find it a bit concerning the speed we're travelling considering the conditions."

"Even though the weather isn't at its finest, I'm glad I came on this voyage, seeing that I was attending other engagements that prevented me from boarding the *Marida* last year. I'm sure, from what I've heard, the two ships are of similar manner anyway."

"So do you find this ship to have luxurious comfort?"

"Yes, indeed."

"It's a pity Henry won't accept any credit due to being part of the guarantee group who designed the two vessels. However, he has expressed an idea that I believe will be successful, and then I'll give him all the credit he deserves."

A frantic dinging bell breaks the night's silence. Only seconds later, a deep, earth-shattering vibration quakes through the ship. The *Neris* stops dead in its travels. A deafening screeching sound comes about, as though the *Neris*'s bow is grinding against something bulky and metallic.

"What happened, dear?" Annie asks in a concerned tone.

Through the fog lays a revealing glowing object. Directly ahead is the port side of the stern, belonging to a large passenger liner.

"It appears we've struck another vessel," Louis bluntly responds.

Annabelle inches dreadfully close to ground zero of the incident. A jumbling mess of metal over the bow's railing is all Annabelle can clearly see through the silhouette fog. She turns around to find Annie tightly holding her husband's hand as he stares out at the vessel. It's like his not wanting to believe in the occurrence of this scenario, judging by his glum expression.

"I need to speak to the captain. Let's go to the bridge."

Annie maintains her grasp as they begin to walk, passing through Louis the ghost along their way. Annabelle's eye releases a small tear while feeling the weight of Louis' sorrow and guilt. He holds out his hand. She moves towards him and grabs hold.

Louis the ghost and Annabelle appear in time to meet up with Louis and Annie on the outer deck section of the bridge. The haunting vision of the moment the two ships hit replays in Annabelle's mind. She quickly turns to Louis while wiping her teary eye.

"I felt your guilt while we were out on deck, and I'm just curious, was the witnessing of the incident is the reason why you did it?"

"That was the tolerant part of the ordeal. I'm afraid that the worst was yet to come."

They enter the wheelhouse on the bridge shortly after past Louis and Annie. Four men are already in this average-size room. A young sailor stands close to the helm. His nervousness is obvious through his wide stare and his fidgeting fingers. Second Officer Thompson is revealing of his nerves. Though the room is quite cool, sweat dampens his forehead under his broad hat, and he can't seem to obtain a firm standing position as he shifts his weight from side to side.

First Officer Monroe is a little more discreet. While wearing a troubled facial expression, he manages to stand solid with his arms straight by his side. Captain Rikes appears different from the others. His slightly slouching body leans against the telegraph as his bloodshot eyes peak out from lazy eyelids. Louis the ghost and Annabelle stand off to the side, ready to observe the commencing conversation.

"Rikes, I need you to stand down as captain, as I am now acting commander of this vessel," Louis calmly says, in a tone suggesting that if he's panicking, he's hiding it well.

"What would you like me to do, sir?" Monroe asks Louis, obviously accepting this arrangement.

"Go down to the lower decks and inspect the damage sustained to the forward bow, and then report back."

"Yes, sir." Monroe walks out.

"Is this your first time witnessing a marine time accident?"

Thompson nods.

"It's OK. The important thing is not to panic. Now, you can go to the wireless operators and find out the status of the vessel we've struck."

"Yes, sir." Thompson walks out.

There seems to be very little reaction from Rikes.

"What gives you the authority to do this?" Rikes says, slurring his words.

"The fact that despite your bad habit, Blue Ocean Line hired you to give you a fair chance. Unfortunately, you failed that chance, and don't bother denying it, because I can smell the liquor."

Rikes keeps his response to the bare minimum. Louis turns to Annie. They hold hands as she gives him a sincere look. Annabelle admires this and interprets it to mean that as long as Louis is by her side, it's OK and she feels safe. Monroe returns.

"The hull at the most forward section of the bow is completely buckled in, which has resulted in a considerable-sized opening."

"Thank you, Monroe."

"It looks like you kept your cool, considering the circumstances," Annabelle says.

"Though it appears that way, I had mixed emotions on the inside," Louis the ghost says.

Thompson returns.

"We've struck the RMS *Mystic*. There's a gaping hole in the starboard hull, and the *Mystic* is taking on water. Also, one of the bulkheads was damaged from the collision."

Annabelle feels a rough tickle in her throat. She relieves it with a quick cough.

"My judgment is we have the ability to stay afloat. I suggest our plan of action should be to open our entrance doors and take on the Mystic's passengers and crew because I gravely believe that ship is going to founder."

Annabelle coughs again this time it's louder and more aggressive, and then she suddenly vanishes into thin air.

CHAPTER 10

Annabelle Delighkan is lying on her side against the cold, hard dock. Harsh, salty seawater runs from her mouth. Once expelling the water and inhaling a deep breath, she rolls onto her back. She immediately finds the two sailors from much earlier kneeling over her, one of which is dripping wet. Annabelle steadily sits up, feeling a little dizzy.

Wanda drops to the ground with weltering eyes and wraps her arms around Annabelle. After a tight grip that seems to last forever, Wanda loosens and pulls away.

"So I suppose you want me to stop scaring you," Annabelle says with a croaky voice.

"That would be nice, thanks," Wanda whimpers.

The sailors bend down and aid Annabelle to her feet. Wanda rises, continuing to attempt to conceal Mitch behind her.

"Are you OK?" the dry sailor asks.

"I'm fine, thank you."

"Seeing that you're too stubborn to go to the hospital to get checked out, we should at least go to the hotel. I booked us all in about a month ago just for tonight."

"OK, let's go." Annabelle begins walking off.

Wanda and Mitch follow. They walk to the end of the dock and then make their way up the street. Approaching the railway crossing in the midst of their travels, Annabelle crosses over it with ease. This makes her question, did she become a ghost, or did she experience something like a dream while really being unconscious? She can't tell.

Arriving at the town garden, Annabelle doesn't notice any change. The abundant crowd continues to munch while they beat to the loud tunes. Heather approaches the two sisters.

"Hey, girls, nice to see you two still about. Why are you wet, Annabelle?"

"Wasn't it raining earlier?" Annabelle sarcastically comments.

"We were just going to the hotel," Wanda says.

"Your father and I are probably going to head off shortly ourselves."

Annabelle suddenly spots Henry a short distance away, among the crowd. Could this answer her question? She intensely stares at him.

"Are you OK?" Heather asks.

Annabelle snaps out of her stare. "I'm fine."

"We might see you girls tomorrow."

The sisters say bye to their mother as she joins the crowd. Annabelle loses sight of Henry. They continue to head towards the hotel. Wanda begins to push through the revolving door.

"I'm going to stay out here for a minute, to catch some fresh air."

Wanda pauses in her revolving motions.

"Don't get any ideas. After your moment of fresh air, I want you in this building."

"Yes, OK."

Wanda, along with Mitch, revolves through the door. Not listening to a single word from her sister, Annabelle darts towards the lively crowd that still occupies the town garden. She almost immediately spots Henry wandering about.

"Annabelle, you look different."

"Have you seen Louis?"

"No, not since he showed you his past memory. Perhaps he crossed over, though I can't be entirely sure."

"You are one clever cookie. Maybe I should Google search the *Neris* and see what else happened."

Loud music beats with the starting of a new song. The crowd acts oblivious to Henry and Annabelle's conversation. She begins making her way out of the crowd and heads to her CR-V in front of the hotel. Henry joins her. She opens the driver's door, reaches in, and pulls out her phone from her handbag on the passenger's floor. Pressing the home button, she sees the device is out of battery charge.

"It's dead, kind of like me these days." Annabelle throws the phone onto the back seat.

Slamming the car door, she looks at the hotel with a little smile.

"Checking into the hotel, sir?"

Henry goes straight through the revolving door, and then Annabelle pushes through it. The lobby is quiet as Pete standing behind the concierge desk is the only one here, making this scene a bit different from earlier.

"Hey, Pete, why aren't you at the party?"

"I was for a while. Then I came back here to prepare myself for the mass of people coming into the hotel I'm guessing all at once, and then I was going to knock off. Say, I don't think I saw you tonight."

"I, uh, took Mitch aboard the *Marida*."

"That's cool. I wish I was going on the voyage tomorrow, but I don't exactly have the finance sorted for that."

"Maybe we should go together. I'm sure it wouldn't be a big issue booking last minute if there are still vacancies and I've got money."

"You would really do that?"

"Why not, I've never been on a voyage before, so it'll be something new and fun."

"Thanks, I agree."

Annabelle walks around in behind the desk. She bends to the bottom shelf, pulls out a laptop, and places it on the desk's surface.

"You keep your laptop here?" Pete questions.

"I thought I was going to take up writing as a hobby." Annabelle flips open the laptop and turns it on.

Henry moves beside Annabelle.

"It's weird that it's suddenly cold in here. Before you came in it felt nice in here," Pete says.

Annabelle subtly smiles as the analogy is convincing enough for her to believe Henry is present indeed as a ghost and not just a figment of her imagination. She swiftly types in her password and then waits for the desktop to load.

"You know, I find the history of Suntree Bay impressive, and it's awesome that you, a Delighkan, solved the legendary mystery. Although you were a little vague with some minor details in your speech."

Annabelle maintains eye contact with the computer screen while listening to Pete. She glides her index finger over the mouse pad and clicks on the internet icon. Clicking into Google she types "Neris" into the search bar. She now opens a Wikipedia page and immediately reads aloud.

"The SS *Neris* was an ocean liner owned by Blue Ocean Line. On March 9, 1912, three days into the maiden voyage, the Neris struck another ship, the RMS *Mystic*, due to heavy fog. The *Mystic* sank, while the *Neris* was towed back to Belfast and later scrapped. Inquires later concluded negligence was the result of the tragedy because it was reported the commander was intoxicated at time of collision. The company, Blue Ocean Line, would dissolve two months later. The *Neris*'s parts, along with her sister, the SS *Marida*, were claimed by the Delighkan family, founders of Suntree Bay, in 1913. The *Neris* went towards construction, whereas the *Marida* remained in service until 1993."

"Wow, the history runs deeper than you think," Pete says.

The telephone rings. Pete answers it. With a confused look, he holds the phone out towards Annabelle.

"I'm not hearing anything except for a bunch of static."

Annabelle grabs the phone and holds it to her ear.

"Now that you know all there is to know, there's one more thing that needs to be carried out before midnight."

"Louis, is that you? Are you calling from heaven?"

"Come to the town garden with Henry."

The call cuts out. Annabelle hangs up the phone.

"What was that?"

"Well, I think my coma has given me the ability to see ghosts and that's who was just on the phone."

"OK, I want to believe you."

"Think of the reason why it felt cold in here after I came in. It's because a ghost is following me."

"That does make sense; the presence of a ghost does make a place cold. Wait, there's a ghost here?"

"Yeah, it's Henry. Anyway, I don't have the time to explain the details now. I'll tell you the full story on the voyage."

"Aunt Anna?"

Annabelle looks beyond the concierge desk to find Mitch standing there. He's wearing shark print flannelette pyjamas and hugging a plush Tyrannosaurus Rex.

"Hey, do your parents know you're wandering about?"

"I was looking for you because we're having a sleepover tonight."

"Thanks, Wanda, for telling me. Well, at least she bathed you."

"It must be great to have a sister who's also a part-time babysitter."

"What's the time?"

"It is quarter to twelve," Pete looks at his watch.

"I've got to go," Annabelle heads towards the revolving door.

"Hey, I think you forgot the definition of 'duty of care.'"

"Come on, boy."

Mitch walks towards his aunty. Henry passes straight through the door.

"I'll see you tomorrow, Annabelle."

"It's a date, see you then."

Annabelle and Mitch push through the door together. Music concludes just as they step out onto the street. Annabelle grabs hold of Mitch's hand and steps over to her CR-V. She opens the back passenger door and aids Mitch into the seat.

"I just need to quickly do something. It should only take a minute or two, so I need you to stay here, OK."

Mitch nods. Annabelle smiles at him and then shuts the car door.

"Did Louis tell you where he was?" Henry asks.

"He must be in amongst all this." Annabelle flays her arm out in the direction of the town garden.

The abundant crowd still occupies this area. She looks over at the stage and then hurriedly approaches it. The band members are disconnecting their equipment and begin tidying up the loose cables. Annabelle quietly hops on stage and stands in the centre, behind the microphone. Hoping to spot Louis from up here doesn't end up being the case. A few people at the front of the crowd draw their attention towards Annabelle. She lightly blows into the microphone and discovers that it's still on.

"I hope everyone enjoyed tonight. From the Delighkan family to you, thank you for joining us in the centenary celebration."

The crowd softly applauds as though only half of the population claps. A sharp noise over the microphone signals its disconnection. Like a group of zombies, the crowd, slowly in an orderly fashion, begins to vacate the area.

Annabelle looks out but still can't find Louis. Henry suddenly appears beside her.

"Sorry, I was admiring the boy."

"That's Mitch, Wanda's kid."

"I vividly remember you at about that age. You don't have any children, do you? I must say, the concierge appears to be a fine gentleman."

"Hold your horses, there. I do like him, but I'm not ready for that whole commitment thing."

"I wasn't implying anything, only observing."

The town garden is finally clear of people, well, live ones anyway. Louis is sitting on the park bench under the gum tree. Annabelle steps off the stage. Henry floats off. They walk in Louis' direction. Annabelle glances up at the clock tower above the library. The time is less than ten minutes until midnight. Passing scattering bits of litter on the ground and a scrappy buffet table, they arrive under the tree.

"You can feel it, can't you?" Louis asks.

"Indeed, it's time," Henry says.

"It's time for what?"

A bright ray of sunlight shines upon the gum tree like the early morning sun peaking above the horizon. The town garden touches the glow while the surrounding buildings remain in the shadows. Eden the ghost steps out through the tree. Her journal is tightly in her grip against her petite chest. Annie the ghost also steps out through the tree. Both ladies approach their husbands. Louis and Henry stare deeply at their wives. Annabelle looks on with a tear in her eye, now realising what it's time for.

"You have the knowledge. Now that it's resolved, we can all finally rest in peace."

"Wait, you can't leave me."

"We'll always live on in your heart. Carry on the Delighkan legacy throughout all of Suntree Bay and while sailing upon the *Marida*. Lastly, make the Delighkan House a lively home again."

"I will." Annabelle smiles over her teary emotion.

The two couples passionately kiss. Annabelle feels the energy from all the love. Louis, Annie, Henry, and Eden all dissolve into a bright white glow, which then becomes a mystic fog. The fog gracefully falls to the ground like misty rain.

Now the town garden is truly vacant with the glowing lanterns and nearby buildings as the only light sources. A feeling of relief washes over Annabelle. Though she's upset to see them leave, she feels at peace knowing that they're no longer in vain. She spots Eden's journal on the park bench. Sitting down, she picks up the journal and curiously opens it to the last page.

September 3, 2013, 23:59

I am so proud of our little Annabelle. Her curiosity and determination shone the light on mysteries none of us had an understanding of. I dearly love Annabelle as the beautiful and upstanding lady she has become. With her heart as big as the ocean and with a free expressive soul, I believe the legacy of Suntree Bay and its delightful tales will always live on.

Annabelle slowly closes the journal and smiles. Her eyelids become heavy as she drifts off into a soothing sleep.

Annabelle peacefully wakes from her refreshing sleep. She looks down to find Mitch against her in a bundling ball, asleep. The warm early morning sun begins to peek above the calm watery horizon. Mitch wiggles as he appears to be still asleep.

"Good morning, Mitch." Annabelle slightly nudges him.

Mitch stretches out his tiny limbs.

"Morning, Aunt Anna," Mitch says with a little yawn.

"Did you sleep well? I know I did."

"That's pretty." Mitch points out to the horizon.

Annabelle and Mitch sit in silence in the serene town garden and admire the welcoming sunrise above the delightfully calm ocean.

Lightning Source UK Ltd.
Milton Keynes UK
UKHW010209081020
371205UK00002B/28/J